# Yesterday's Shadow

P.J. Murphy

ISBN: 978-1-3999-7287-1 (Paperback edition)

ISBN: 978-1-3999-7286-4 (E-book edition)

# Contents

# Foreword

It wasn't my intention to publish my novels in reverse order. *Troubleshot* (my fourth novel) preceded *Dead Letters* (my third), and you hold in your hands my second. For a long time, I didn't plan to publish *Yesterday's Shadow* at all. I sent it off to a few agents after finishing it back in 2007, but I quickly abandoned that attempt. Although it was fiction, the novel was too personal, and I worried that parts of it could be misinterpreted.

*Yesterday's Shadow* was a bit of a reaction against trends in contemporary literature. Every book I picked up was about another culture or period, something inherently different and more interesting than life in the country I lived in. I wanted to write something about the ordinary – or our individual versions of the ordinary, and what happens when they intersect. I didn't want to fashion the plot around the hero's journey, either. I wanted my protagonist to be relatively passive throughout the story. One of the novel's themes is the consequences of inaction and how that's a choice in itself.

It was hardly likely to set the publishing world aflame with excitement.

When *Dead Letters* did well for itself, I mentioned to a few readers that I had two further unpublished novels knocking around. I teased *Yesterday's Shadow* in December 2022, publishing an extract of the New Year's party section on my blog. It garnered a lot of interest. Eventually, I agreed to share the novel to get a second opinion about whether it was worth doing anything more with – but only after I had brushed it up a little first. I approached this with some reluctance. I wanted to move forward with my writing, not look backwards.

Returning to *Yesterday's Shadow* was like revisiting my adolescence. There is so much of me in it: my (non) relationship with my father, my exploration of Christianity and its history, and my experiences trying to make sense of the world around the turn of the millennium. Pretty quickly, it had its hooks in me again. I wanted to improve the writing, but more than that, I became overwhelmed by the melancholy of nostalgia. I've always had a weakness for it. I realised, too, that I didn't want to consign those parts of me I had invested in this novel to purgatory on a dusty hard drive.

I hope that reading *Yesterday's Shadow* brings you something near the same level of experience that it brought me. At the very least, it's a record of the early steps of a writer finding his voice. Maybe now, I can step out of its shadow.

P.J. Murphy, August 2023

# Chapter 1

## *Act Like a Man*

They fought most nights. I lay in bed, not moving, barely breathing. My father's voice rattled the doorframe, sometimes deep and threatening but most often sharp and violent. Mum rarely spoke. When she did, her voice was so fragile that I could barely hear it.

For a long time, I tried not to think about what was happening in the living room below. I closed my eyes and pretended it was just the TV. Ours wasn't the warmest of families, but I was sure my mother and father loved each other. It couldn't be them fighting like that.

I stopped trying to fool myself after I noticed Mum's bruises. I must have been fourteen at the time, in the spring of 1998. Mum usually wore long-sleeved tops, even when it was boiling hot outside, but every now and then, she got careless. She rolled up her sleeves once to do the washing up, and there were purple finger marks just below her elbows. Another time, she winced when I hugged her around the waist. Whenever I questioned her, she found something else to talk about. I soon grew accustomed to following her lead. She was a brick wall to me when it came to that. She would never let me in, never admit weakness or accept my help.

We carried on like that for well over a year.

As an adult, I've thought a lot about why I played along with all this. I don't have a good answer. A teenage growth spurt meant that I could look my father level in the eye, but I was nowhere near feeling able to challenge him. I feel as much a culprit now as he was. It wasn't fear or apathy that stopped me from acting; it was etiquette. My father saved his outbursts until nighttime. The violence was contained, separated from family life. To bring it up during a family dinner, however chilly, seemed somehow terribly wrong. Our culture equips us only for comfortable, regular little routines. I couldn't find a way into that tumultuous private life of theirs.

But I worried. I would lie in bed, staring at the ceiling, imagining what was happening below. A big part of me wanted to go down there and tell them to stop it, but whenever I pulled back the covers, I was overcome with shivers, as though an arctic breeze had squeezed through the window. Eventually, I stopped trying to get to sleep while my parents were up. I turned on my bedside lamp and tucked into a book. I read for hours, often well past midnight, until I could hear my father snoring. During those years, I gained my interest in science fiction: in the novels of Philip K Dick, Frank Herbert and Douglas Adams, to name a few. I read to escape my world. The earth became only one planet in trillions. Its concerns were insignificant.

Life continued like that for shamefully long. The days' routine of school, homework, and then TV ran parallel to my parents' regular arguments. Life was so rhythmic, so predictable. It felt like it would go on this way forever. The beatings my mother endured seemed hardly to matter. They were accepted; they were mundane.

Then, on 29th October 1999, everything changed.

* * *

It was a Friday night. Other kids my age were hanging around on street corners or trying out their fake IDs with bouncers at *Wetherspoons*. I had just given up on my homework. Mum had a rule that I wasn't allowed to play on the computer or go out with friends until I had finished, and since I was in the second year of my GCSEs – an exam year – I rarely got to do much else. My brain was on overload. I couldn't face another textbook, so I headed downstairs, where my parents were watching TV. They spent whole evenings doing that, even when there was nothing decent on. I think just being able to focus on moving images helped them to avoid arguing with each other. Relations between them only became strained when the TV was switched off.

I knelt beside the sofa and whispered 'goodnight' into Mum's ear. I dared not disturb my father from whatever rubbish he was watching. I crept back upstairs, brushed my teeth and got into bed.

The heating was still on, and the boiler was working overtime because Cambridge feels its winters hard. I tucked myself in, hermetically sealing the edges from drafts. I was so tired that I didn't reach for the novel I was reading; I just turned the light out and closed my eyes.

Before long, my thoughts stopped buzzing, and I began to drift off.

I snapped open my eyes. Time had passed, but I had no idea how much. It was still dark. It wasn't morning.

'What the hell is that supposed to mean?'

My father's voice was impossibly loud.

I slipped an arm from under the sheets and reached for my bedside lamp. Something stopped me from turning it on. Maybe I didn't want to acknowledge that I had heard anything; maybe I thought that whatever it was would blow over if I stayed there in the dark, breathing shallowly. But my father was so close. The landing light was on. I could see his feet breaking the strip of light between the door and the floor, just like in horror films when the killer is about to grab the handle.

'Well, what do you want me to do?' my father shouted again. I couldn't make out what Mum had said to him. She must have been at the bottom of the stairs. 'No, I will not come back down. This is my house!'

Then, a few seconds later: 'Don't tell me what to do, Angela!'

I closed my eyes, but it continued. I heard Mum climb the stairs. She was tiptoeing, trying not to wake me. My father thundered across the landing.

A minute later, something thudded against the wall. One of the pictures I had arranged on my bookshelf fell and cracked against the corner of my desk.

Another thud. Plaster crumbled, falling as dust. This house seemed flimsy, pitted against my father's rage.

Mum squeaked, and something dropped to the ground.

This was it. I had to do something. I threw off my sheets, marched to the door and flung it open.

The build-up to this moment had lasted years, but it still didn't prepare me for what I saw.

My parents were at the top of the stairs, in front of the airing cupboard. My father towered above Mum, who lay in a heap against the wall. Her face was pale, streaked with tears, and her body was crumpled, but her gaze was firm. She was almost scowling at him, a hardness I had not seen in her before, although her bottom lip quivered. I'll never forget that image: him there, nostrils flaring, all beast and sinew, with victory in his bloodshot eyes; her so vulnerable and yet defiant. His fists were clenched. Muscles flexed beneath his skin.

Muted, second-hand violence had become brutal reality. There was no hiding from it now.

Mum was the first to spot me. Her eyes lowered from my father and turned to me.

'Look at me when I'm talking to you!' my father shouted.

'Go to bed, Nick,' Mum told me.

My father wheeled around to face me. 'Listen to your mother. This is none of your business.'

I took a step back, overwhelmed by his size and sheer ferocity. There was no way I could face him. I had seen plenty of violence on TV, but that wasn't real. It was certainly nothing like this.

But I had to do something. I couldn't pretend I hadn't seen this. I glanced at my mother. She was shaking her head. Her eyes pleaded for me to go back into my room. But I couldn't move. I was rooted to the spot. Whether through bravery or cowardice, I was a part of this now.

I opened my mouth, but I didn't know what to say. I wanted to tell him to stop. I wanted to tell him to leave us alone, that he was a monster, but those words were heavy; they came from so deep within that my tongue hadn't the strength to handle them. My throat constricted. I knew what was coming next. My breaths had already started to shallow to sobs.

'What are you doing?' my father said, advancing on me.

'I thought you were a man. You're sixteen, for Christ's sake! Act like a man!'

I wanted to; I really did. I didn't understand why I was crying, but I couldn't stop now. I began to retreat back into my room, but my father caught me by the arm.

'Where do you think you're going? You can't even stand up for yourself. Look at me when I'm talking to you!'

My father grabbed me by the chin and forced me to face him.

'Let go of him!' screamed Mum.

My father looked at me with disgust and tossed me aside. I don't think he cared where he threw me. My mouth smacked against the door frame as I fell. The impact turned it numb at first, but I tasted blood. I touched my lip with my fingers, and sure enough, I was bleeding. My head started to spin.

For a few seconds, nothing happened.

My father loomed above me. I looked up at him fearfully, anticipating the next blow, intentional this time. But his bearing had softened. His eyes were wide, and his lips formed vowels. Explanations. Excuses. He didn't object when Mum pushed past.

'Nick,' she said desperately. 'Nick, are you all right?'

I nodded groggily.

'Come on,' she said, helping me to my feet. 'Let's get some ice on that.'

Mum barely said a word whilst she nursed me. She put me to bed and fetched some frozen peas, which she wrapped in a towel and pressed onto my face. She told me my teeth were all okay and that I would heal. I didn't say anything, didn't complain that I was at risk of being suffocated by vegetables. I just wanted to go to sleep.

I'm not sure where my father went, but I didn't see him

again the rest of the night, except in my head, in that grotesque pose looming above my crumpled mother. I couldn't get away from it. That image would come to haunt me. Even now, years later, if I let my thoughts stray, I find myself back there, a useless boy stupefied by reality.

* * *

I was born with a heart condition called *aortic stenosis*, where the valve between the left side of the heart and the aorta is narrowed, making it difficult for my heart to pump blood out to the rest of my body. If I hadn't had surgery when I was younger, I would probably have the heart of an old man by now and would be practically guaranteed to have a heart attack before the age of thirty. Even at sixteen, I had to monitor what I did. I shouldn't really have pushed myself as hard as I did sometimes. Although the valve opening has been widened, it's still deformed. In time, I might need an artificial valve.

Pretty crap, really.

There are some benefits, though. I have a cool scar that earned me serious respect at school. Plus, I got to skip sports and spend the free period in the library. If I'd have wanted to, I could probably have got all of my homework done during school hours, but I tended to get hooked on one book or another and spent the bulk of my spare time reading. I got through David Eddings' epic, *Belgariad*, in a matter of days (an achievement I still recall with pride).

My heart condition was one of the main reasons my parents stayed together as long as they did. It gave them something other than work to talk about. This was no bad thing considering that my father hated his job, and that his eyes used to flash nastily whenever Mum mentioned hers (it was always a sore point that hers paid the higher wage). My condition gave my mother something to worry about every time I lost colour, and this, I imagine, gave her something else to dwell on other than her own predicament.

She was sitting beside my bed when I woke. Her hand held mine limply, but this became uncomfortable with time. I gathered the will to move my fingers, hoping she would get the hint and let me go. Nothing happened.

I opened my eyes, peeling my lashes apart. The clock on my dressing table read 8:35 a.m. Mum's head hung forward. The chain earrings she wore brushed against her cheeks.

The house was silent except for my mother's breathing. Not a car passed by outside. It seemed as though the world was waiting for something. Even the birds didn't dare to sing.

That's how I knew that everything was about to change.

I pulled my hand away. Mum woke.

'Nick.' She lifted her head and massaged her neck. 'You're awake.'

'So are you,' I said.

I was a teenager, remember? She was lucky to get that much out of me.

'How are you doing?' She grabbed my hand again.

'Okay.' I fidgeted. My bones clicked.

Mum leaned forward to examine my lip. The wound was superficial, hardly noticeable, with the blood wiped away. Mum's eyes were puffy. She wore yesterday's clothing, and her dark hair, still tied back, had begun to prise itself loose.

'Where's Dad?' I asked.

'In bed, last time I checked,' Mum said.

'Listen, Mum,' I said, 'I was going to go out later. Sam's invited us over for war-gaming. Is that okay?'

I've thought a lot about why I changed the subject like that. Stranger things happened in the following days, but I believe it requires explanation. I put it down to the part of me that wanted to forget all about what had happened and carry on as normal. I was fully aware that this would not be possible, but this didn't stop me from trying.

If I could relive that moment, I would probably say something different because it set the tone for my relationship with my mother.

'Hmm.'

Mum was miles away. She got up and walked to the window, looking out at the morning. I watched her for a while. With the light behind her, I could see my mother as she would have appeared when she'd been my age. She seemed so pensive, so unsure of herself, like someone just setting out in the world. Gone was her confidence. For the first time – just for an instant – I think I understood her, conceived of her as someone for whom marriage and motherhood were simply a period of life. She had been called Angela far longer than she'd been called Mum. The family life I had always taken for granted was just an era for her that was drawing inexorably to an end.

'Why do I have to do this?' Her back was still turned to me.

I had no answer.

Mum came and knelt beside my bed. She clasped both of her hands around mine and lowered her head.

'I don't want to do this now,' she whispered. 'Not right after last night. I wish there were another way.'

'What is it, Mum?' I said softly.

'Your father and I have been growing apart for some time,' she said, more loudly now. Her words were rehearsed. 'Sometimes, when people live with each other every day for years, they get used to each other. Being together becomes less special.'

'You're getting a divorce?'

Mum nodded but couldn't speak.

'This is because he hurt me, isn't it?'

A panicked expression shot across Mum's face. 'No, Nick, no. This isn't anything to do with you. You can't blame yourself for this.'

But that wasn't my concern. I was already well ahead of her:

'Who am I going to live with?'

'It's up to you,' Mum replied.

'Are you going to keep the house, or is Dad?'

'I don't know, Nick. We haven't discussed that yet.'

Mum turned away. It was then that I realised.

'You haven't told him?'

'Well, no. I wanted to talk to you first. I wanted to make sure you'd be okay with it.'

Would I be okay with it? Why wouldn't I be? Was she expecting me to cry or something? I had no feelings for my father. For that matter, I had no discernible feelings about anything whatsoever. Everything seemed distant. Why wasn't I upset? Love, hate and pain, these were all emotions experienced by other people, not me.

'I'll be fine, Mum,' I said.

# Chapter 2

## Other People's Worlds

This isn't a book about abuse. There are already whole libraries full of those, recounting stories far more shocking than mine. It's disgusting what human beings can do to those closest to them. I don't feel qualified to present my tale as anything like theirs. What Mum and I experienced at my father's hands isn't news. It happens often to many of us. It shouldn't, but it does.

I started my story this way because I had to. It's not something I can ignore. It framed everything that followed. I had entered another world where the rules had changed, and anything could happen. I could look back at my life until that point as though it had been lived by another person. That chapter had been closed, sealed tight, preserved, done.

I reflected on this as I made my way to Sam's house.

The city of Cambridge has a history to it. I'm not just talking about the stuff that inhabits the libraries and lecture halls. There's plenty of that, for sure, but for anyone who's grown up there, it's just the backdrop – the architecture, the scholarly taste to the air and an explanation for the absurd road layout. No, the history that truly assaults me in Cambridge is my own. The city, ancient and modern, has played host to events that have shaped me, constructing pathways in my brain that will govern my behaviour for life.

Silly things like the supermarket we shopped in every week now hold tremendous significance to me. They have extended the store since I was sixteen, and shuffled the aisle layout around to keep regular customers on their toes. Going there is like visiting a friend you haven't seen in years and being struck less by what about them is the same as what has changed. I remember my family doing our usual Saturday morning supermarket run just hours after that fight. It turned out to be our final outing. My parents were still officially 'together'. It was the strangest experience watching my mother act like nothing had happened. I couldn't forget what she had told me, couldn't remove it from the forefront of my mind. Everything about my family now had an expiry date. Would my father leave before the milk curdled or the quiche sprouted mould? Every word we said to each other, every glance or small courtesy, seemed futile, for it served only to delay the unveiling of the truth that all of this would end. We lived in yesterday's shadow.

I was relieved to get away after lunch. My friend Sam had roped me into an afternoon of tabletop wargaming. I was less into this by that point in my adolescence, but I was grateful for any opportunity to get out of the house. Sam lived on the other side of town, in a big place beside the railway tracks. The same prim-and-proper type neighbourhood as ours, but the houses were a few years older.

I packed my army figurines into a box, tucked that into my rucksack, and began the hike there.

The sun was bright, so the walk itself was pleasant

enough, freshened by the morning's rain. The pavements were still dark with moisture, and water droplets hung like fairy lights on still branches. The cold made the cut on my lip sting. It was swollen. I worried for a moment that my friends might notice the wound, but then I recognised my mistake, attributing them with any level of observational skills. No, this secret would remain my own.

I took the route through the city centre, along King's Parade and Trinity Street, past the centuries-old colleges infiltrated by cafes and chain stores. It was Saturday, so I contended with crowds of shoppers and tourists. Avoiding them would have entailed too much of a detour.

I got to Sam's at around half past one. Our group often met there because his house was the only one with sufficient floor space and parents obliging enough to flee to a garden centre for the afternoon, leaving us to set up our battlefields in the front room. I don't ever remember seeing Sam's parents once in all the times I went there. Maybe I've blocked them out. I find it difficult to imagine him originating from anywhere.

Sam styled himself a non-conformist. This entailed him dying his hair black, getting an ear pierced and wearing nail varnish. In every other way – including, perhaps, this – he conformed to the normalities of being a teenage boy. He spent most of his time trying to make himself look clever. He *was* clever, but even now, I have trouble admitting it; such was my aversion to how he shoved it down everyone's throat.

When I arrived, he was talking about an *Advanced Dungeons and Dragons* campaign (or *AD&D*, as he referred to it) he had devised. He didn't interrupt his flow to let me in, just gestured with a tilt of his head that I should enter.

'So then, right,' he shouted down the hall to the living

room, where his audience was listening, doubtless with bated breath, 'you end up going back into the same dungeon you've just come out of, but because you've got the thief with you now, you can get through the door with the silver crest and...'

I set up my army as he continued. I had been paired with Brian and his goblins, battling over a strategically important bit of carpet. Sam hovered over us, still monologuing about his campaign. His troops had been ready for an hour, but we were still waiting for the fourth member of our party.

'You're a bit heavy on the archers, aren't you?' Brian commented. Sam had gone off to get drinks, affording us a few seconds of relief. 'You know, you can't possibly win through bow-fire alone. My foot troops are ten-a-penny, and you'll never get past my boar riders' armour.'

Brian delighted in offering tactical advice. I often reacted to this by doing the exact opposite of what he said. He had warned me about his cavalry before, but that had only increased my resolve to destroy them utterly.

Thirty minutes later, it was still just the three of us, and half of my troops had been massacred. Brian was doing some kind of weird victory dance involving obscene pelvic manoeuvres and chanting, *'Oh yeah, oh yeah!'* This was the most energetic I had seen him in months. Brian wasn't the most active of individuals. The part of his body that got the most exercise was probably his 'gaming hand', which had turned claw-like from his *Nintendo* controller. Intensive video gaming had restricted his social skills, but he would occasionally betray a level of intelligence wasted on the accumulation of trivia. I felt sure that he would end up as a comic book shop owner.

Much as my friends irritated me, it was a relief to get

back to normal, to be with people who didn't know or care what had happened the night before. This was the world I was used to. Already, my parents' fight seemed like an aberration. Nothing was going to change; nothing ever did. Apart from my swollen lip (which, as predicted, neither had remarked on), there was no evidence that anything had happened.

Brian and I were about forty minutes into our battle when the phone rang. Sam got up to answer it. I tried to listen in, but Brian and I were in the throes of a rules dispute.

'*What's up, Michael?*' I heard Sam say.

'Look,' Brian said. 'They're not in your line of sight. You need to take a panic test.'

'*Oh, come on, Michael, this keeps happening!*'

'Are you going to take it or not?'

'*None of them know what they want,*' Sam said. '*That's part of being female.*'

'Hello? Nick!' Brian thrust the rulebook in my face, pointing a finger to one of the sections. 'Just accept it and roll the dice.'

I took the dice and rolled them without question. This resulted in my general and his elite bodyguard fleeing for their lives. Brian clapped with delight.

When Sam returned, he was shaking his head and muttering to himself. I cast him a quizzical glance, but he declined to offer up any information. If you know something that others don't, you don't just give it away just like that. Well, Sam didn't, anyway.

'Listen up, guys,' he said after a while. 'Are you free tonight?'

Brian and I glanced at each other.

'Is this Michael-related?' I ventured.

'He's got issues.' Sam sat back in his armchair and adjusted the oversized *Nirvana* t-shirt. 'He's currently spending the day with Tess, trying to convince her that he's the one for her. He's paranoid she's cheating on him. I've said I'll go to this party with them tonight, keep an eye on her and report back. I could use your eyes, too.'

Let me interject with a couple of things here. Firstly, I must acknowledge that teenage relationships are only of interest to other teenagers – particularly when viewed from the male perspective. Let me venture a guess as to why: something about teenage boys is just, well, disgusting. It's off-putting to view them in any kind of romantic context. At the time, these relationships felt mature and vital. Looking back, we were just copying how we thought adult relationships worked until habit and history had made those behaviours our own.

The second thing I want to acknowledge is how quickly Sam discarded all the rubbish that typically occupied his mind to focus on stuff that really interested him: people. Despite all the pretence, he was a true gossip at heart.

'Come on, Nick,' Brian said. 'It'll be fun. We'll survey the scene – a bit of reconnaissance. It'll be top secret. Like Tom Cruise in *Mission: Impossible*, only easier to follow.'

I was less keen. I couldn't deny that I found it fascinating, this close-up view of a relationship. I had seen Tess and Michael together countless times before, tugging at each other's sleeves and exchanging saliva. Somehow, I had never managed to imagine myself that comfortable with anyone. This was my opportunity to get a glimpse of what it might be like. But going to a party? The price was too high.

Still, what was the alternative – go back home and face up to what was happening with my parents? What if they fought again?

So, I agreed to go.

Sam quickly devised a plan of action. We would all stay at his place until the appointed hour. He ordered in pizza. I phoned Mum to tell her, and she was fine about it. She seemed pleased to have me out of the house.

We passed the time watching *Babylon 5*, specifically the episode in which Sheridan leaps into the chasm, embracing death on *Z'ha'Dum*. It was one of our favourite sci-fi moments, rivalled only by the emotional punch of the last-ever *Quantum Leap*. By the time the opening credits appeared on screen, I had been sucked into yet another world.

* * *

On a Saturday night at the end of the century, I found myself waiting in the cold outside the front door of 129 Lincoln Avenue, home of Mr and Mrs Geoffrey Duverman. They had gone to Paris for a romantic weekend, thereby granting implicit permission for their daughter to invite people around in their droves. Michael and Tess were already inside, having arrived early to help our host, Anna, get the place ready (i.e., move anything remotely valuable into the garage).

Anna opened the door, exposing us to the dulcet tones of the *Spice Girls*. Yes, I know, ask most people to come up with a playlist for a party in the late nineties, and *Spice Girls* will probably top the list, but that was honestly what was playing. There was a good reason why certain music became synonymous with that period: it was *everywhere*.

I cringed. I trust it goes without saying that manufactured pop wasn't my thing. It didn't appear to be Sam's either, judging by the gagging noise he was making.

'Come in,' said Anna, casting us a cursory glance with her bleached blue eyes.

Michael was an acceptable part of her world because he was going out with Tess. The rest of us had no such VIP status. How that irritated me! It wasn't as if she didn't know who I was – we were in the same science group. She used to sit at the back of my chemistry class, glancing at herself in a fold-out mirror. She always gave the impression that she wasn't taking anything in. Her grades indicated otherwise.

Anna showed us around the place disinterestedly, then left us to our own devices. The Duvermans' house was perfect for parties (although I'm not sure Anna's parents would have agreed had anyone asked them personally). It was one of the newer buildings in Cambridge, situated on the outskirts near Addenbrooks. It consisted of three floors of unnecessarily large rooms, a balcony and an outdoor swimming pool, which had wisely been placed out of bounds (although I'm told that a film of vomit was discovered floating there the following morning).

The front room had been cleared of everything except the stereo system, and transformed into a dance floor, where the most brave or tipsy of my peers were already strutting their stuff. The music was deafening. Even out in the hallway, I feared for my eardrums. The kitchen was the first room on the left. We deposited our bottles there as payment for the night's entertainment.

'What's the plan?' I asked, pouring myself some coke.

I was there for a reason, and it certainly wasn't to have fun.

Sam grinned. 'Just chill, Nick. Enjoy the party and play it by ear.'

'No problem.' I downed my coke, as most normal people might a shot of vodka. It didn't have the same intoxicating effect, although the bubbles that frothed in my nostrils did have a kick to them.

Most of my year's 'trendy' people turned up that night, bearing loud voices and an inflated sense of self. They didn't say hello to me, and I didn't talk to them. Both sides seemed content with this arrangement. I didn't usually speak to people outside my friendship group. Ours was an exclusive club, insular, accessible only to those who had watched the last episode of *Farscape* or *Stargate*. We were just as proud that we weren't like the 'trendy' sixteen-year-olds as they were about not being us.

I can't deny that I admired them in some small way, though. Smalltalk came so easily to them. Outside the classroom, I had little to say.

My group of friends had a particular way of talking to each other. You couldn't really call it conversation: our communication could better be described as bouts of speaking. We spoke to each other in statements and only about subjects on which we considered ourselves authorities. What one of us talked about rarely bore any relation to what the previous person had said. One minute, Brian might be talking about one of the bosses in *Resident Evil*; the next, Sam would be going on about the finer points of Asimov's *psychohistory*. It was like we were all there alone, in little vacuums. The only common theme was that nothing we discussed was in any sense real. It was all TV and fantasy worlds. All our ideas came from other people; they had been sold to us.

Brian and I camped out in the dining room, which adjoined the kitchen, affording us a view of the new arrivals. Sam, who was far more at ease with this than the rest of us, started chatting with a group of girls from his psychology class.

We sipped at our drinks without exchanging a word. I'm not sure what we were waiting for. We started playing tiddlywinks, flicking discarded bottle tops into the fruit bowl. Brian thrashed me, as he always did with anything vaguely competitive.

The evening did have one highlight: Anna's sister, Jo, was there. I knew her from chess club. Jo was a year younger than us and the complete opposite of her sister. She was a bit of a loner, virtue of her ability to insult people unintentionally. Her hair was a muddy blonde that night. She dyed it often. I never understood why: the colour never stuck, and the chemicals made her hair frizzy. But she was all right, Jo. She was a girl, but you could talk to her.

'Hi,' she said when she saw us looking at her.

Brian and I nodded back, playing it cool.

Jo fixed herself an orange juice from the fridge before joining us at the dining table.

'I swear Anna plans these parties to coincide with my coursework,' she said as she sat down next to me. 'Invites all her loser friends over. And you lot, for some inexplicable reason.'

'We're not invited,' Brian tapped the side of his nose. 'We're not even officially here.'

Jo turned her back to Brian. 'So, what are you doing here? This doesn't seem like your kind of scene.'

'Trying out new things,' I replied. 'Meeting new people.'

'Don't tell me you're over Lara?' Jo laughed. 'Venturing out into the real world!'

Ridiculous though it sounds, I blushed. *Lara Croft* was my first love. Not all that more unobtainable than most of the non-computer-generated girls I knew.

'What happened to your lip?' Jo said before I could come up with a response.

I touched it with my fingers. 'It was an accident.'

Jo frowned. She laid a hand on my shoulder and tilted my face until she got a better view in the light.

'What happened?'

'Just mucking around,' I said. 'Caught it on a bedpost.'

'It's swollen. It must sting like hell. Listen, we've got some ice in the freezer if you want some.'

'No,' I said quickly, remembering how trigger-happy Mum had been with the frozen peas the night before.

At this point, Brian sneezed incredibly loudly. Jo jumped out of her skin, spilling a few drops of her drink onto the table.

'Sorry about that,' Brian said, snorting mucus back into his nostrils.

'Um, well, I'd better go,' Jo said shakily. 'I've got loads of stuff to get through. Humphreys wants a piece on agriculture in Ghana, and Andrews wants to know about the role of clothing in Macbeth – "Um, they wear it!"'

'Good luck,' I said.

Brian had a massive grin on his face as Jo left. I ignored him as best I could.

'She fancies you, you know?' he said, undeterred.

'No, she doesn't.'

'She does.' Brian nodded knowingly. 'I pick up on these things. I've seen how girls act around my brother. They like the athletic type. They pretend they're all 'I don't care', but the moment he says anything at all, they start giggling. I'll tell you what gives Jo away, though: her tits.'

I took a sip of my drink and looked away. I hated that word, 'tits.' Clearly, they were central to the teenage experience and were the main reason why we watched *Xena*, but the word itself sounded so dirty. If only there were a more polite way of referring to them. 'Boobs' sounded even worse. 'Knockers' was just plain wrong. For some reason, I only came up with the word 'breasts' some time afterwards.

'Girls' tits do things,' Brian continued. 'They don't just sit there.'

Now, I was preoccupied with the idea of breasts (or whatever they were) getting up and performing everyday household tasks, like making the tea or emptying the dishwasher.

'When girls are aroused, their tits inflate,' Brian explained. 'Y'know, sexually. Girls see a potential mate and start producing milk for offspring. They can't help it. I'll tell you what, Jo's tits were inflating like hot air balloons. You should have seen them from the side!'

I won't describe here the gestures he made while saying all this.

I gulped down my drink and set about attempting to erase from memory everything that Brian had just told me.

And the evening wore on.

Nothing is more likely to distance you from your peers than sobriety. Go to a party like that, and you'll understand why. As the hours leapt to double figures, the music we endured underwent a metamorphosis. At about half nine, disposable pop became rock, then garage, then trance. Around eleven, the volume dropped. I doubt, somehow, that this was due to anyone responding to the neighbours' complaints; it was far more likely due to pounding alcohol-induced headaches. People stopped talking to each other. Everybody just stared into space, mourning the high that had passed. Shortly afterwards, someone had the revolutionary idea of putting the rock music back on, and the drunken chanting began.

It was about then that Brian headed home, leaving me to go look for someone else I knew. I hadn't seen Jo again, so I searched for Sam and Michael. I was supposed to be helping them out, after all. I found them in the front room. Sam was passed out on the sofa. Michael was quite conscious. He was sitting on an armchair near the conservatory doors, where the air was frozen but fresh. Tess was lying across his lap. One of her arms was wrapped around his neck. The other grasped a bottle of *Bacardi*.

I waved to Michael. Immediately, he slipped out from under Tess and got to his feet, pausing as an afterthought to give her a little peck on the cheek. Tess wasn't content with half-measures, however. She grabbed the back of his head and kissed him firmly, thrusting her tongue through her chicken wire braces and into his mouth.

I looked away until the act was done.

Michael was the first in our group to have a girlfriend. I still hadn't got used to it. I couldn't work out how it had happened either. He epitomised a teenager suffering the worst effects of hormonal change. His skin was angry with acne, and a growth spurt had stripped all the muscle from him. He walked around stooped, seemingly ashamed of his height. Still, Tess allowed him to hold her hand in public and kiss her, even though it made the rest of us cringe. Something about him must have impressed her. He did know the lyrics of every Bob Dylan song ever written. Perhaps that was it.

'I didn't realise you were still around,' he said. He sounded tired and decidedly sober. 'If I'd have known...'

'It's okay,' I said. 'I've been keeping Brian company in the kitchen.'

'That sounds like something you'd do.' He scratched his nose. 'Listen, I think I'm going to go in a minute. Tess wants to stay, but I've had enough. Can I offer you my floor?'

I glanced at Tess and realised how useless I was. I had come there, supposedly to help my friend, and had spent the whole party hiding away. The time for espionage was over. Tess' head was tilted back over the arm of the chair. Her mouth was wide, gaping at the ceiling. Her breaths were half snores, half gurgles. Nothing would be happening in that neck of the woods any time soon.

'Thanks,' I said, 'but my Mum offered to come and get me.'

That was the idea, anyway. The problem was that no one picked up when I called home a few minutes later. I let the phone ring for ages, but nothing. I sat in the hall with the receiver pressed against one ear and a hand cupped over the other. Michael stood beside me. At first, he refused to leave until someone answered, but after five minutes of persuasion, he was out the door. He wanted out of there more urgently than I did by that point, I think.

I know it was stupid of me making him go, but I couldn't have someone there looking over my shoulder. Something was definitely wrong. Mum was usually so reliable. She would never leave me to walk home at night: I was still a baby in her eyes. I started to think again about my parents' fight and all its possible repercussions.

I gave up phoning home ten minutes after Michael left. I put the phone down and removed my hand from my other ear, to which it had been pressing tight to give me a chance of hearing the phone over the music. Emerging from my private drama, I tried to regain my bearings. The house was like a battlefield. There were groaning bodies littered awkwardly wherever I stepped.

I felt less in awe of these social animals now that their

alcohol had failed them. The stuff fuelled their confidence. They looked a lot less impressive, passed out on the floor, stinking of sweat.

I grabbed my coat and headed for the front door. Nobody noticed me go. The last ones standing were all out in the back garden singing *Wonderwall*.

That was the world I came from when I met Peter.

# Chapter 3

## *Encounter*

It was a long walk home, and I was woefully unprepared for the weather. The cold came as a shock to my system, which had spent the previous few hours within the stifling heat and sweat-dampened walls of Anna's house. I was at least two layers short of retaining some semblance of warmth. I shivered from the inside out as though my body was objecting to my stupidity from its very core.

I distracted myself by conjuring up progressively more unpleasant scenarios of what might be happening at home. What if my father had hurt her? What if he had really hurt her?

I forced myself to count my footsteps, making rhythms out of them. Pretty soon, this lost its appeal. I then took to contemplating how my shadow darkened, lengthened and faded as I strode beneath streetlamps, before comparing a vandalised speed camera to a felled machine from *The Empire Strikes Back.*

In desperation, I called home again from a phone box on Hills Road. Still no answer. This was getting silly. I was still quite far from the city centre. I could have phoned Michael then and there and told him that I had changed my mind and wanted to stay at his after all, but I opted instead to continue my great doomed trek. I had a point to make. I'm not sure what that point was or who I was making it to. All I kept hearing, over and over, was my father shouting, *'I thought you were a man. You're sixteen, for Christ's sake! Act like a man!'* Each step I took was a gesture of defiance.

It must have been around half-past eleven when I reached St Andrews Street, just beyond Emmanuel College. This was my least favourite part of town. By day, it was packed full of traffic, with buses carting people to and from Addenbrooks and the train station. You literally had to fight your way along the thin pavement through groups of students so engrossed in a debate about classical thought or metaphysics that they were oblivious to anyone coming the other way. Cyclists buzzed up and down. Pedestrians with sensory overload stepped out in front of them, causing them to swerve into vehicles, greeted by a torrent of horns and expletives.

That night, all of this was gone. Down at the taxi rank, seven or eight cabs waited for people to come out of the clubs. The *Burger King* across the road had closed sometime earlier. Streetlights drenched the townhouse style buildings in bronze. All windows were dark. I quickened my pace.

There was an overhang above the shop front of *Robert Sayle*, the department store. They've ripped the site down now and constructed a shiny new shopping centre, but back then, it was common to see beggars there – it was a lucrative spot, a prime location from which to ambush visitors on their way to the bus station. I always found it best to keep walking and pretend they weren't there. That's what I did that night. I walked on past the man in the crumpled coat and tattered scarf. He wasn't looking at me and didn't have a collecting bowl or a cardboard sign asking for money.

That should have been me on my way. But then I heard him utter, 'Save me.'

His voice was weak, but that wasn't what made me stop: it was the words themselves. This wasn't a plea for loose change, or pity, or whatever message might be best placed to trouble my conscience. This was someone facing their doom.

I stood there, fighting with myself. I wasn't far from home by that point – another fifteen minutes or so until I could be in the warm. But I knew I would think about him out there while I snuggled up in bed. Living in Cambridge, you teach yourself to be immune to pleas for charity. So much of it is organised rings; you don't know who you can trust. Something about this man pierced through all that. I couldn't get the image out of my head of him slumped there. I had to make sure that he was all right.

I approached cautiously. The old man's body was still. His cheeks were pale. It was as though he had been cast in marble. His back was propped up against the shop front. His head drooped towards his right shoulder, and his eyes had slipped shut.

I leaned close, careful not to touch him.

*Please, just ask me for money, and I'll know you're like all the rest.*

I thought back to years earlier, when my elder cousin used to play dead. I remembered prodding him and making stupid noises, trying to make him wince or laugh, but he never once did. He would wait until I was on the cusp of panic before springing to life. This was different. You get a sense of when a situation is serious. The rest of the world quietens for a moment.

I focused on the whiskers on the man's upper lip, waiting for them to move. Reluctantly, they did. Little wisps of condensing air escaped his nostrils. Faint, so faint.

I stepped back, willing myself to keep on walking, to just pretend I hadn't seen anything. He had fallen asleep, that was all. Uttering the words, 'Save me.' Perfectly normal.

If I left him alone, he might die out there in the cold, and the thought of that would haunt me for the rest of my life.

I looked around. Get help. Let someone else deal with it. Then I heard my father's voice again: *You're sixteen, for Christ's sake! Act like a man!*

I drew in a breath and steeled myself. 'Hello?'

It wasn't loud enough to rouse him.

I forced myself to crouch back down. I reached out a hand and shook him. His body was cold to the touch. For a moment, I thought it was too late, but then, slowly, his eyes creaked open.

At first, the man's gaze was unfocused. As the seconds passed, he appeared to make sense of what he was seeing. Reason awakened in the darkness behind his pupils.

'Are you alright?' I asked.

The old man didn't reply. He just looked at me and slowly cracked his lips into a smile.

Then he closed his eyes and fell back asleep.

'No! No!' I cried, tugging at his arm, all inhibitions crumbling. 'Wake up!'

I looked around desperately. The street was still empty. I caught a glimpse of a young couple, arm in arm, but a second later, they disappeared around the corner, trailing behind them the click of heels.

'This is who He sent?' the man murmured.

I turned back to him, but his eyes were still closed. He didn't smell of alcohol; otherwise, I would have taken him for a drunk.

'What?' I shouted. 'What did you say?'

I shook him until he woke, luring him to his feet with the promise of a hot drink. I don't know what I was thinking. I didn't have a clue what it was like to live on the streets, yet I had convinced myself that I was the only one who could help this man. This was to be the most important thing I would ever do.

I made him walk with me, reasoning that the exercise would get his blood circulating. *McDonald's* was only open for take-outs that time of night, so I went in and bought him some coffee and one of those hot apple pies they do. I stayed with him to make sure he ate it all.

It was drizzling, so we took shelter beneath a market stall canopy outside Town Hall. The square was full of those stalls, dormant then but set up to accommodate fruit and veg, ethnic clothing and CD racks during the daylight hours. We weren't the only occupants. I could hear movement nearby, couples kissing, inebriated partygoers whimpering, and drug dealers offering various substances.

There were quite a few people around that part of town, students mainly, but there were also a lot of locals pouring out of the nightclubs. They queued up at the burger vans on either side of Market Square, and occasional tussles broke out. A couple of women with goose-bumped legs were shrieking and clawing at each other in the middle of the street. I watched them, fascinated, while my companion wiped syrup from his beard.

I glanced at him occasionally as we sat there on a disused table. We didn't talk. He concentrated all his effort on eating. He did this carefully, methodically, with little sign of pleasure. He needed that food, though. With a few glances, a few blurred snapshots, I observed how skeletal he was. His neck was the giveaway – all veins and ligaments, no flesh to it at all. His off-white beard alone afforded it some substance.

He began to cough, doubling up with convulsions. I didn't know what to do. Was I supposed to clobber him on the back? Then, I realised that the coughs were too shallow to clear anything from his throat. No, he was sobbing. There were no tears, but his face said it all, a mask of pain. The creases in his skin had deepened into dark gouges.

I didn't know what to do. I could hardly get up and leave him like this, no matter how much I wanted to, but I couldn't think of any way to comfort him, either. So, I just sat there and waited, peering out through the stalls at the activity beyond, trying to distract myself from what was happening next to me.

Eventually, he stopped, and I asked, 'Are you okay?'

The old man grinned crookedly. 'I'm ready if that's what you mean.'

His voice was husky, trampled into the ground, but there was a certainty to it.

I looked away. How was I supposed to get out of this now? I could only imagine what Mum would say if she found out about this: '*No good deed goes unpunished,*' or something of that ilk.

When I dared to look back, the man was smiling at me. It was genuine this time. There was kindness, sympathy even, in his weather-beaten face.

'What's your name?' he asked softly.

I opened my mouth, and at first, no sound came out. Then, 'I'm Nick. Nick Farlowe.'

The old man nodded. He crunched the cardboard packaging from his apple pie into a ball.

'My given name is Peter. You can call me Peter.'

'Thanks.'

'What are you doing out here, Nick? Someone your age shouldn't be out this late. Especially on his own.'

'Lucky for you, I was.'

Peter scratched his beard. 'I suppose so.'

This was the closest I ever got to thanks.

We sat on the unused market table and looked at each other for a few minutes, each waiting for the other to speak, but neither of us had anything more to say. Peter appeared to be deep in thought. Once or twice, he muttered to himself.

Then, the college clocks struck midnight.

'Listen,' I said, checking my watch. 'My parents are waiting up for me. I'd better go.'

'Of course,' Peter said. 'Go home.'

That was all the blessing I needed. Somehow, that was enough to convince myself that my buying him a hot drink and a bite to eat would make enough of a difference that he might survive the night. I didn't question it. I just backed off and walked away.

I hurried the rest of the way, making the final stretch in record time. As I turned into my street, I saw the police car.

# Chapter 4

## *Aftermath*

The neighbours called the police. It was too much for them to have their TV shows interrupted two nights in a row. At least, that was the explanation Mum gave me.

A few days later, I overheard Mrs Dickinson talking to the white-haired lady from number 16. She said she had made the call after hearing china smashing. It just so happened that she was the proud owner of the largest collection of teapots in the Northern Hemisphere. It was anyone's guess whether she'd been most concerned about my mother or the crockery.

Whatever the truth, the police had arrived to find Mum barricaded in the bathroom, nursing a bloody nose. This alone was evidence that it had been a bad fight: my father never usually hit her anywhere so visible. After letting the police in, he had returned to pleading through the door, attempting to coax her out as though they weren't there. I can hear his voice now, that mixture of desperation and menace. When one officer had touched him on the shoulder, trying to get him to back down, he had taken a swing at him.

My father was now down at the station, 'cooling-off' in one of the cells.

Mum told me all this across the kitchen table, but not before berating me for not calling. She didn't believe me when I told her I had phoned several times until we discovered that my father had disconnected the phone from the socket. She was more subdued after that.

The house was eerily quiet. Mum held the same bag of peas to her face that she'd used on me the night before. She spoke with a hushed voice, quite possibly because she didn't want to be heard by the police officer sweeping up the remains of the plates that had – so the story went – 'accidentally fallen off the draining board'.

I took hold of Mum's hand as she reached the end of her story. 'You told him, then?'

Mum didn't answer. She glanced distractedly at the WPC.

'We're okay now,' Mum said when their eyes made contact. 'Thanks. Thanks so much.'

The WPC – Louise, I think her name was – set aside the dustpan and brush. 'That's all cleared up for you, Angela. Will you be all right on your own?'

'I'm not on my own. I've got my son with me.'

'Okay. We'll be in touch. What happens next depends on you, Angela. I want you to consider what we talked about earlier.' For some reason, she glanced at me as she said that. 'Would you like us to let you know when we release your husband?'

'No,' Mum said quickly. She breathed in deep. 'I don't want to know.'

Louise nodded and smiled like she had seen this sort of

thing a thousand times before. Sadly, she probably had. Then she grabbed her coat off the back of a chair and made for the front door.

Mum got up and saw her out. Then she went to the window to watch through the net curtains. Several minutes passed before the police car finally drove off.

'I thought we'd never be rid of her,' Mum said, turning back to me. 'It didn't have to turn out like this. It wouldn't have if it weren't for the bloody neighbours sticking their noses where they don't belong!' She paused. 'God, what must they think?'

'I don't care about that, Mum,' I said.

She still hadn't answered my question. Had she told him? Had she asked my father for a divorce? All my senses told me that she had – that this had been the trigger for the outburst – but I still needed it confirmed, rock solid.

'Well, I do!' Mum snapped before peeping back through the curtains. 'This is a respectable neighbourhood.'

We each thought about this for a few seconds. The clock on the wall ticked. My muscles were buzzing with energy, and my sinuses tingled.

For the second time that week, I caught a glimpse of a younger version of my mother. It seems odd that it happened at that moment, for she was acting more middle-aged than ever. Still, the years peeled away before my eyes until she was seventeen again, with bold lipstick and long hair in tight curls. I was looking onto the disco floor where my parents met. Images from *Saturday Night Fever* kept leaping to mind. A Gloria Gaynor song sounded in my ears. The seventies were way before my time, so these were my sole references. At what point did Angela stop being a girl and become someone with a house to keep, someone who could be held to higher standards? Had I done that to her through the sheer act of being born?

Mum stared at the hole my father had kicked in the door a few weeks earlier. He had plastered it over but hadn't gotten around to giving it a new coat of paint. She then surveyed the thin, grease-tarred wallpaper behind the hob and traced the line of ornamental geese down to the family pictures from holidays past.

She looked up with a start.

'Do you fancy coming to church with me, Nick?'

I was raised a Christian. When I was younger, Mum went in for it big-time. She sent me to a Church of England primary school. The irony is that she wasn't particularly religious. I had never seen her do the sign of the cross on herself or read the Bible anywhere outside church, and at times she was pretty free with her profanities. I'm convinced that the sole reason Mum introduced me to Christianity was because she felt it was her duty as a responsible mother. Christianity represented morality. It was something you associated with families of good repute.

We hadn't been to church in years, not since my grandfather died. That would have been just after I started secondary school. Actually, we stopped going before his death. It was on Sundays that we went to visit him in the hospice. God could wait, but my grandfather had only months. We never got back into the habit of going to church after that; we never seemed to have any incentive. Mum only ever went when she was troubled.

Before that, we used to go every week. It was tedious. The hymns could be cool once you got to know them, but the sermons, oh, the sermons! I developed an armoury of coping strategies to get me through, but none ever worked for more than five minutes. There were only so many animal shapes I could contort my fingers into.

I could always tell that it wasn't just me suffering. People cough when they're bored. It's easier to notice that tickle in your throat when there's nothing to take your mind off it. They coughed like anything during those sermons. Sometimes, I sat there with my ears primed, ready to track coughs from stall to stall like the demon travelling in that Denzel Washington film. I took guesses at who would be next. Would it be the lady rooting for a tissue in her handbag or the man with the pockmarked face and greying hair already raising a hand to his mouth?

I wasn't old enough for the sermons to register, anyway. I'm not saying that young people can't understand religion, not at all. Faith is faith. If anything, it's easier to accept stuff when you're younger and less set in your ways. But sermons are different. They take for granted an adult view of life and its intricacies. Some of us get to a fair age before death intrudes or we realise what people are really like. How can you possibly understand the entirety of what the clergy has to say about sin and service to God if you haven't touched oblivion or become fully aware of the spectrum of awful things that human beings do to each other? The vicar's words appealed to experiences I'd never had and lessons I had never learned.

I did my bit, though. I learned the New Testament inside-out. I could tell you exactly how many baskets of breadcrumbs were collected after Jesus fed the five thousand, and I could pick out every one of the discrepancies between the gospels. Even at the age of nine, I felt the stirrings of a desire to know alternative realities inside out. I studied the Bible years before I came across Tolkien's *Middle Earth* and Asimov's *Galactic Empire*, but my approach was roughly the same. I tried to step out of my world and place myself in a land I had never seen, governed by customs that were almost totally alien. I don't think the church would have approved of this approach, but it wasn't as if I would ever end up a priest. There were two major obstacles to this: the first was that I didn't understand half of what I read, and the second was that I couldn't persuade myself to believe.

I didn't think about any of this in church with Mum that Sunday morning. The only thing that occupied me was my current reality: I was an only child whose parents were splitting up.

I watched Mum throughout the entire service. She was quiet and tearful, barely able to sing. I held her hand as we prayed. I can remember praying for world peace. I was aware that this was a cop-out, but I wasn't sure enough about anything closer to home to know what to wish for.

As I thought about it, I realised that I wasn't actually all that upset about the idea of my father leaving. I don't think I ever really loved him; we didn't have that much of a connection. When I thought about him, I saw a self-pitying man who had a habit of throwing his weight around, exploiting what little power he had.

I just hated seeing my mother like that.

What had kept her with my father so long? Genuine love, fear of being alone, or a steadfast belief in the textbook family life that had been sold to us? In public, Mum always projected the image of a professional woman whose affairs were in order. Not that morning. Her sniffs carried, reflecting off the stone walls. Everybody could hear them.

We were in the back pews of the church of St Andrew

and St Mary in Grantchester, the next village upriver from Cambridge. It was a small church, very village-oriented, with a certain homespun warmth to it. The wooden pews creaked whenever you moved. They were softened by hand-made cushions with cross-stitch covers depicting biblical scenes, the pride of a dedicated parishioner. It felt less like a church sometimes than a grandmother's front room. Everyone there was elderly, and tea and biscuits were always available after the service.

I noticed concerned, embarrassed glances from several of the congregation.

I recognised quite a few of the faces from my childhood, like memories from a past life. One woman approached me the moment communion finished. I recalled that her name was Primrose and that she was a churchwarden and a stalwart of the parish council. She had stuck in my mind because she used to make Sunday mornings endurable by sneaking me boiled sweets.

'I haven't seen you in years, Nick!' she said, catching me as I stood up. 'My, you've grown!'

She ushered me towards the rear of the church, where refreshments had been set out. I didn't take my eyes off Mum. She hadn't budged from the pews.

'Tell me how you're doing,' Primrose said, stepping sideways to obstruct my view. 'Breaking all the girls' hearts?'

I shrugged. I wasn't in any mood to be patronised.

'A little bird tells me you've been doing well in school,' Primrose continued. 'That's what I like to hear. We always knew you were a clever lad.'

'Thank you,' I mumbled.

'You've got a bright future ahead of you. No doubt about it. How old must you be now? Fifteen? Sixteen? Have you worked out what you want to do with your life yet?'

'Not yet.'

It was about time I was getting back to my mother. She needed me.

Primrose glanced over her shoulder. As she did so, I got another glimpse of my mother. The vicar had sat down next to her. He was talking to her softly, resting one arm on the back of the pew just behind her.

'Plenty of time to decide. You're still young.' Primrose rummaged in her handbag. 'Sherbet lemon?'

* * *

We got out of there about an hour later.

'Lovely people,' Mum said as she drove us home. 'They mean well.'

I crunched on a sweet.

* * *

I spent most of that evening online. This was a bit of a treat. Mum was in charge of the dial-up connection, and she normally only allowed me to use the internet for a maximum of half an hour each day. Mum forgot about this that night. She must have had more important things going on in her head. She spent hours on the other line, phoning with friends and family.

Dad didn't come back. Not even a phone call (not that he would have got through, anyway). The house assumed its now-customary silence.

Michael was online too, so I chatted over MSN Messenger for a while. I didn't tell him anything about what had happened since the party. Instead, his own problems dominated. I knew it was bad when he told me he had *Blood on the Tracks* on in the background.

'Is that Bob Dylan's breakup album?' I typed. I had never listened to it, but Michael recommended it to me often enough that it felt almost like I had.

'Yup.'

'What happened?'

'We had an argument,' typed Michael. 'She says I'm paranoid. Do you think I'm paranoid?'

I thought back to the epic failure of our surveillance operation that previous night. I had no evidence with which to make any kind of judgement whatsoever, but I was inclined to distrust Tess. She wasn't one of us. She didn't live by our rules.

'I'm so stupid!' Michael continued. 'I confronted her. I drove her to this. I could have gone on living in denial, and we'd still be together.'

'That doesn't sound like a sound basis for a long-term relationship.'

I love it when people give you the opportunity to sound wise when you actually know nothing at all. Still, I did wish I had something more useful to say. My friend was hurting.

More than that, Michael and Tess' relationship had become an institution. It had lasted less than six months, but that seemed a lifetime in those days. It seems silly to compare it with my parents, but right then, both stories seemed an indicator of a broader trend. All the couples I knew were turning against each other. No relationship had a future. Maybe if Michael and Tess could get through this, there might be hope for the rest of them.

Was that what I wanted to happen with my parents? Despite everything, did I want them to get back together? I kept telling myself we would be better off without my father, but that didn't explain why everything seemed so bleak. If Mum gave him another chance, safeguarded with ultimatums, might things work out?

Michael's next message blinked on the screen:

'I guess we'll never know.'

I stared at those words for some time, until the letters burned the back of my eyes. Neither of us wrote anything more that night.

# Chapter 5

*The Preacher*

I got up at seven the next day, drained and numb. Mum had left for work about an hour earlier, so the house was empty. I poured myself some cereal and munched it down, barely tasting it. My spoon clinked against the bowl as I scooped up the remains of the milk. It was the loneliest sound I had ever heard.

I then packed my bag and headed out of the front door.

It was one of those drab, wet mornings that deprives everything of colour – entirely in keeping with a Monday. As usual, the Cambridge traffic was stationary, so crossing roads was easy enough. I joined the flow of school blazers making their way through town.

So, this was the beginning of my first week without my father. It seemed inappropriate to carry on as though nothing had happened that weekend, packing my stuff and heading off to school like any normal week. How could I continue the pretence that nothing had changed? The school timetable didn't care about that. I had no choice but to comply.

As I got closer to school, I became nameless, a mere product on a conveyor belt.

* * *

'You are absolutely crap today,' Jo said as she took my rook. 'Worse than usual, if that's possible.'

I glanced around the chessboard, trying to disguise my surprise. 'Just lulling you into a false sense of security.'

'I have to say I'm feeling pretty secure right now. Let me give you some time to consider my predicament. I'll be back in a minute. You had better not move any pieces.'

And Jo went off, presumably to the toilet. Socially awkward though I was, I realised it wouldn't be polite to seek clarification on that point.

Brian wandered over. He had defeated his own opponent in five minutes flat and was now doing the rounds, monitoring the other games in progress. He looked down at my board critically, jutting out his lower lip.

'You're screwed, Nick,' he said. 'Totally screwed.'

'Hmm,' I said.

'Why do you always insist on using the English opening? You need to have a bit more of a clue what you're doing before you sacrifice the centre of the board like that.'

'Call it chivalry.'

Brian thought about this for a moment. He had a worrying look in his eyes, so I braced myself for one of his usual cringe-inducing comments about me and Jo. Brian was nothing if not predictable, and I had asked for it, I supposed.

He caught me by surprise when he asked, 'Are you coming swimming tonight?'

I hadn't considered our swimming trips. How would

they work if my father wasn't coming back? He would pick me up afterwards, but I couldn't rely on that anymore. I didn't relish the idea of another nighttime walk through Cambridge's winter wonderland. And when did Mum expect me back? She worked in London and didn't usually get home until late. We hadn't talked about that. Neither of us had considered how my father's leaving affected our schedules.

A stubborn side of me kicked in then. Why should I change my plans? Besides, I didn't fancy going home to an empty house. Okay, so I usually spent most of the evening shut away in my room, but that wasn't the point.

'Sure,' I told Brian. 'I'll come.'

A few minutes later, Jo returned to find Brian occupying her seat, revelling in the illusion that he was thrashing me. She gave him the swiftest of glances and shooed him out of her way.

'I'm sure you didn't have that knight when I left,' she said, sitting down.

'If I'd have cheated, I'd have given myself a queen.' I didn't have much of a sense of humour that day.

'I can still mate you in three.'

Behind her, Brian sniggered.

'Rubbish,' I said, although I knew she was probably right.

Jo proceeded to demonstrate. She ended her display by kicking my king over with her queen.

'Girl power!'

You could say that without irony back then.

I stared forlornly at the board, at all those useless pieces.

Jo got out her packed lunch. 'So, what are you enduring this afternoon? Maths and Biology?'

'You have a good memory. Don't expect me to know what you've got.'

'History (urgh!). And English – the role of clothing in Macbeth, remember? I was doing it while my house was being trashed. Do you know what I found out? Clothes are a metaphor for how we hide our true selves: our thoughts, our feelings.' Jo looked me straight in the eye. 'We never say what we really feel.'

I matched her gaze as long as I could, but in the end, I had to look away.

Brian was choking on his sandwich.

It's human nature to chart our lives by major events. Where were you when they shot Kennedy? Can you remember the fall of the Berlin Wall or footage of the Gulf War on the news? I've never understood this preoccupation with dates. Birthdays, anniversaries, deaths, invasions and capitulations are all a blur to me. It's not as though I've never lived through anything major (i.e., involving a conspiracy theory). Take the death of Princess Diana as an example. I remember footage of the wrecked car, and I'll never forget the crowds of people piling up flowers outside Buckingham Palace and weeping as though they had lost their own daughter. I know it happened before the events I'm writing about in this book, but I couldn't tell you what year. I'm not sure what today's date is, either, or when my grandfather finally succumbed to heart disease. I'm a calendrical void (yes, it is a real word). I can't order my life around arbitrary measurements of time.

How does this relate to anything? The point I'm trying to make is that, for me, it isn't major events that usher in a new age so much as their aftermath. I've only worked out the exact date of my parents' separation by plotting events between then and Christmas, tracing backwards. In a sense, the date itself was less significant than what happened in the days and weeks that followed when, for the first time, for better or worse, I was without my father. I had to fit into a reality where I didn't have two parents at home. The numbness that had been dogging me gave way to an unfathomable sadness. I couldn't tell you where it came from, but it was all-encompassing. I couldn't share it with anyone, so I kept it close to my heart.

As the melancholy took hold, it became harder to speak. I had to force every word out. Eye contact grew painful. Nothing, and no one, seemed right. All because of this secret I was keeping, all because I had to play the role of a student getting on with his life. I had to give the appearance of coping.

By the time we went swimming, all I wanted to do was go home and lie in bed, staring at the ceiling, not thinking about anything. I spent the entire time sinking to the bottom of the pool, breathing out until my lungs were empty, and all I could hear was a deep industrial hum and my body screaming at me. Colours were smears, and human bodies were vague outlines tinted chlorine blue. Underwater, all my thoughts took second place to my body's need for oxygen. It's good sometimes to remind yourself that you're an animal, that no matter what kind of life you lead, you're still a victim to the basest of needs. Everything becomes much simpler when you look at it that way.

The only problem was that I had to surface every now and then, and Brian was always there waiting for me.

'Forty-five seconds,' he counted as I wiped my eyes and gasped for breath. 'A fair effort, I suppose. Especially since you're not all that fit. My brother stayed under for over five minutes the other week.'

I spluttered a bit. Brian took this to be my contribution to the conversation.

'You don't have the lungs for it, that's all,' he continued. 'You need to practice, build up capacity. That's what Adam does. He comes down here every day. Sometimes, he lies in bed at night, holding his breath.'

Adam was there, in fact. Brian's brother was one of the lone 'professional' swimmers doing lengths over the other side of the pool, unapproachable behind his dark goggles.

Brian proceeded to assail me with further stories about his brother. Apparently, Adam had been headhunted as an extra on the set of *The Beach* but refused because he thought Leonardo di Caprio looked like a girl.

As soon as I could, I dunked myself back underwater.

The next time I surfaced, Brian was timing his brother. When Adam reached our end of the pool, Brian shouted out his length time, along with a few words of encouragement. Adam ignored him. He took his breathers at the other end of the pool and never looked in our direction.

'He's just focused,' Brian explained.

I said nothing.

'Adam's practising for the trials next weekend,' Brian told me later. 'Big national competition he needs to qualify for. Mum has changed his diet especially. We're on pasta all this week. Anyway, my father's away on business, so there's space in the car. We're going to make a day of it. Fancy tagging along?'

'Where?' I asked, trying to buy myself time to think up an excuse not to go.

'Here.'

This caught me off guard. I had expected it to be somewhere more exotic, like Peterborough or King's Lynn. Brian had mentioned space in a car, after all. Why drive into Cambridge? Surely, that was more trouble than it was worth. For some people, I supposed, driving was still the default.

Confusion, as much as anything, made me say 'yes'.

Shortly after that, Sam and Michael swam over. The group then started talking about the usual stuff. I couldn't say what it was: I wasn't really listening. I drifted away, surveying the pool, which was packed to capacity. The racket was unbelievable: water gushing out of the flume, people diving, lifeguards whistling, and everyone shouting to be heard over the din. The shallow end was filled with parents accompanying water-wing-clad children who bobbed up and down like Brussels sprouts in a saucepan. Elsewhere, teenagers dive-bombed each other. A girl shrieked as her boyfriend splashed water on her face. It was hardly the most appropriate venue for our meetings, but it was tradition now.

'I know why Michael's quiet today, but you had better explain yourself.'

Sam had followed me away from the group.

'I'm fine,' I said. Then, to deflect, I added, 'How about you?'

'Fine.'

I dunked myself back underwater. By the time I resurfaced, Sam was back with the others.

At six o'clock, a woman instructed everyone wearing a green wristband to leave the pool. We pulled ourselves up onto land and pattered over to the changing rooms. We didn't speak or look at each other as we showered and dressed. None of us were truly comfortable in our skins.

When we were done, we waited for each other in the

cafeteria. Sam took ten times longer to get ready than the rest of us. He always spent ages on his hair. I'm not sure why we waited because we each went our separate ways once outside. Sam unchained his bike, nodded goodbye and was off. He raced down Mill Road, cycling without holding onto the handlebars. I had never been able to do that. My life flashed before my eyes each time I tried.

Michael walked back, and Brian waited for his Mum to pick him up.

I was on foot, too, but I didn't head the same way as Michael. I mentioned earlier that my father used to pick me up from swimming. That's not strictly true because it implies effort on his part. The truth was I just used to catch a ride with him. My father always met me in the Hog's Head, a few minutes' walk away. It was a nice pub, quite old, my father's local. He liked it, he told me, because it was 'one of the few places in this town that isn't full of students.'

He always arrived before me and was never late. Again, I should contextualise this to avoid painting an inaccurately positive impression. My father worked as a forklift operator at Manfred and Hans, a printing warehouse in Sawston industrial estate. All day long, he hauled massive loads with his little vehicle, feeding the conveyor belt quires to bind and filling the bellies of trucks that spat and spluttered black muck across the loading bay. His was a lonely job, of servitude to machines that bellowed their authority, barring workers from the power of speech. The only thing that kept him going was a thirst for a pint or three when the day was up. He was always the first to clock off when five o'clock eased in. He then hurried to his car and sped off to the pub. Fortunately for me, the location of his drinking spot and his time of arrival coincided with my swimming pool sessions. We were always home long before Mum returned from work. I'm not sure she even knew we spent the early evenings down the pub.

I could see the Hog's Head from outside the swimming pool. I wondered if my father was inside. Was he missing us, sobbing into his drink, or was he joking with his mates?

My lip stung. The chlorine in the water had opened it up again. Strangely enough, I hadn't noticed before then. I realised as I stood there how angry I was with my father. Not just about the fight – it was stronger than that – and it didn't seem new, either. It was like it had been there all along in the background, unacknowledged. I didn't want to speak to him, but maybe it would help if I saw him. Maybe seeing him there and turning my back on him, making a conscious decision to do it, rather than just having him disappear the way he had, maybe that would bring closure. I could move on from that.

I followed the pavement around Parker's Piece. I could have cut right across it, but I didn't like the look of that. Parker's Piece is basically a big lawn crisscrossed with cement paths. In summer, it's the centre point of the community, crammed with sunbathers, cricketers, volleyball matches and frisbee throwers. That evening, it was pitch black. The grimy streetlights didn't penetrate far through the trees, whose branches still bore withered leaves and the occasional horse chestnut. There were only a couple of ornamental-style lamps in the centre of the green itself, evoking Jack the Ripper's London.

The longer route took me around the circumference and down Regent's Terrace, a back alley lined with parked cars and bins for dog waste.

A little way away, Mill Road was clogged with traffic, but it was eerily quiet at the park's edge. I passed a couple of women at the traffic lights, but that was it. As I approached the corner of Parker's Piece, the Catholic church up ahead stood black against the orange sky.

A man was standing on the corner by the public toilets. I could hear his voice from way off. At first, I thought he was talking on a mobile phone, but he was way too loud for that. He was projecting his speech as though addressing a large audience, but nobody else was there. As I got closer, I began to make out the words:

'...and a man came forward, and he said to me that he did not know if he believed in the Lord, but that he lived his life as best he could. He was a moral man, hard-working; he loved his wife and children, and even took them to church. He asked me if he would be saved when the time came. I looked at him, and I could not disguise my pity. "My son," I said to him. "Answer me these questions, and you will know your fate. Have you ever lied, even once, even if it's a white lie or to save another's face? Have you ever stolen anything? The value is irrelevant. Have you ever looked at another person with lust? Christ said, '*whosoever looketh on a woman to lust after her hath committed adultery with her already in his heart.*'"'

The preacher's words were slow, and there were long silences in the middle of his sentences as he drew in breath. A casual observer might conclude from this that it was all unplanned, all spur of the moment. Listening closer, however, it was clear that this man knew exactly what he was saying. He had rehearsed it all. Every word followed, definitely and precisely, from the last, like a puzzle completing itself. Clearly, he knew the greater sum of his message, but he was in no hurry to get there. Nobody was listening. Not apart from me.

I quickened my pace. I hated going past those public toilets at the best of times, having heard all manner of horror stories about the goings-on inside. The branches clawed at the streetlight above.

The preacher continued, 'The man lowered his head and said, "Yes, my conscience tells me that I have done all these things," and at once, he realised – just as we all must – that leading a good life is not enough. We will be condemned as sinners on the Day of Judgement. And he got down on his knees, and he begged me to save him. "You must put your trust in Jesus Christ as your lord and saviour," I told him. "You must repent of your sins and enter into the service of Christ."'

I had almost passed by. If I didn't look up, maybe the preacher wouldn't pay me attention. But there was nobody else around. It wasn't as though he could fail to notice me.

'My friend,' the preacher said as I neared.

Instinctively, I looked at him. I didn't want to, but I couldn't stop myself.

I recognised that face. The man in the street, the man I had saved two days earlier.

'Peter?'

The preacher looked startled. I'm not sure why he didn't recognise me; it should have been the other way around. I hadn't changed, but this was a different Peter from before. He seemed more robust now, invigorated. His face was formidable, and his eyes burned with intensity. Still, beneath this, I could see that he was physically weak and malnourished. The worn jumper and the discoloured jeans he wore loose around his skeleton emulated flesh, but a gust of wind pressed the material to his bones and shattered the illusion.

Peter lowered his voice to a normal level. 'The Good Samaritan.'

I couldn't read anything into that tone. It was neutral. A statement of fact.

I coughed and looked away.

'Do not be ashamed,' Peter said. 'You see now my true nature, just as I see yours.'

'Are you okay?' I asked. This man was intimidating, but I was pleased to see him, if only to have confirmed that he had survived the night.

'You ask only because you cannot see beyond filthy, sickly flesh,' Peter said. 'Spiritually, I am healthier than ever; that is all that truly counts. I am following my path, laid out for me by our Lord Jesus Christ, just as He does for all of us.'

I studied Peter's lined face for a few moments. Part of me wanted to flee; another was keen to discover whether it was wisdom or insanity that lurked behind his eyes.

Peter was examining me, too. He was the first to speak.

'I have something I want to give you.'

'Oh no,' I said, 'I can't accept...'

He thrust a book into my hands.

'You saved me. Now, I must save you. Take it, read from it, let it be your guide.'

I looked down at the gold-leaf lettering on the cover. It was the New Testament. The cover was unblemished. It was in a better state than anything I would have associated with this man.

I tried to give it back. Peter refused.

'One week is all I ask. Read it and accept the Lord into your life. If it's not for you, return it to me, and I will accept it.'

I held the book loosely, barely able to summon the enthusiasm to keep it in my grasp. I couldn't drop it, either. Politesse prevented that, and fear of how Peter might react.

'Promise me you'll read it,' Peter insisted. 'For your soul's sake, please promise me.'

I nodded, then turned and walked away. It was the easy way out. At least, that's how it felt at that moment. I kept going and didn't look back.

As I passed the Hog's Head, I peered inside. No sign of my father. Somehow, that seemed less important than before.

# Chapter 6

## *The First Lesson*

As the week continued, it sucked me in. Wednesday was the low point between the two weekends; Thursday, a slight improvement, but only because we didn't have French; and Friday, a whole week since my parents' fight. That week saw a solidification of life without him. Dust settled, habits formed, and routines rejigged. In time, we would each accept the new texture of our lives.

Mum worked late every night that week, so we hardly had time to catch up. I was convinced that she stayed in the office just to avoid having to answer my questions. When she got home, at around half-eight or nine o'clock, she locked herself in her bedroom. I don't think she went to sleep most of the time, though. Every now and then, I heard her play a Tracy Chapman record on her stereo. She needed space. I respected that. I turned on the radio and carried on with whatever I was doing. I didn't bother her, and she didn't bother me.

I didn't hear anything from my father. If he phoned, Mum never mentioned it.

My relationship with my friends continued largely unchanged. The distance was already there. Sam had clearly noticed that something was up, though, and he approached me a couple of times to ask how I was. I kept quiet and skipped our next swimming trip.

I was no happier alone in that house. I couldn't concentrate on my homework, and my parents weren't there to force me into it. I passed my time brooding. I spent hours flicking through the TV channels, but there was only so much of it I could stomach. I kept coming across things that annoyed me: celebrity chefs, *Dawson's Creek* and adverts for shampoos and anti-ageing creams. I could feel my brain rotting away. One night, I got sick of it all. I went upstairs and threw myself on my bed. I lay for a while in the dark.

I usually spent the early evenings in the pub, where I would set up with my homework away from the smoke and sip on a coke whilst reading about osmosis or matrix theory. Nothing stopped me from doing the same at home (it was a far more suitable environment, in fact), but I just didn't want to. It all seemed so pointless. All this work was supposed to help set me up for life, but honestly, if you do well at school, what does that give you? The opportunity to do well at college and then at university. Then what? A job, bringing in enough to survive on. Working to live and living to work.

I sat up and switched on the light, looking for something to distract me from these thoughts. I glanced over at my *PlayStation*, but I already had a bit of a headache from the TV. My eyes scanned my bedroom shelves, passing *The Silmarillion* and *His Dark Materials* until they settled upon a volume that didn't belong there. It was hard-backed, with no dust cover, no illustration. Its title stood for itself. Peter's Bible.

I reached for it. This was the first time I had touched it since dumping it there days earlier. I would have to return it to Peter sometime. Stealing a homeless man's Bible would be, well, a bit low. It occurred to me that I had better make some sort of effort to read it. I couldn't put this off forever.

I flipped open the front cover. 'New Testament, King James Edition'. There was a logo stamped just below the title, and the name and address of the Zionist church.

I turned the page and began to read. The pages were thin and rippled, like a beach at low tide. Several passages were accompanied by notes – commentary, interpretation – presumably Peter's. I read some of these but skipped over most. The writing was tiny and often unintelligible.

And that was it. That's how I started reading the Bible again.

It was the strangest thing going back to the Bible, years after I had last been to church. It was kind of like revisiting an uncompleted thought. As I read, familiar avenues of enquiry opened to me. I found Matthew's Gospel fascinating. Christ's charisma was wholly evident despite the plain language, diluted by translation after translation. At times, He was talking directly to me: '*Ask, and it shall be given to you; seek and ye shall find; knock, and it shall be opened unto you. For every one that asketh receiveth; and he that seeketh findeth; and to him who that knocketh, it shall be opened.*' He was waiting for me and a billion other lost souls. He needed only my permission to enter my life.

All this still seemed crazy. I couldn't reconcile it with the real world. And yet, I couldn't cast Peter out of my mind. There was something about him, his whole being. He was like no one I had ever met, a spirit that didn't belong in this stagnant, decaying world. I had to adjust my concept of reality to incorporate him. Where did that leave me? More to the point, if I could recognise Peter's existence, how much more of a stretch would it be to incorporate Christ into my reality, too?

I hadn't thought about that stuff in years, not since Mum had stopped taking me to church, not since I had met the people I regarded as my friends. But Christianity had left its traces in me. I had never quite let go of its architecture of explication.

Over the next few days, I read the Bible a lot. As I did, Christ's words triggered something inside me. I felt this urgency to learn how to lead my life properly. It was clear that I had been doing something wrong. Christ offered a better explanation of what that was than anybody else.

No, it was more than that.

I kept thinking about Peter. His faith was so strong that he could impose it on strangers. Who was I to dismiss that? If someone believed in something that strongly, it had to have some truth to it. All these years, I had prided myself on having an open mind. In practice, that had just entailed me avoiding thinking about life, death, and God at all. I couldn't allow that to continue now that I had met Peter.

Sooner or later, I had to go back and return that book to him. I knew he would grill me about what I had read, and I can't deny that this made me nervous. But it was also exciting. I felt sure that he could understand things I couldn't.

It was dark when I went to meet him after school. It hadn't yet turned frosty, but the moisture in the air made the chill oppressive. It was the kind of weather that saps your life force away. The late summer sunsets we had enjoyed barely three months earlier seemed but a fantasy. Long gone were the days of thunder bugs and dry grass, of colour splashed across land and sky, bleeding into one at the horizon. The days now were grey, empty and sparsely populated with life that did not flourish; the best it could hope for was to endure.

Peter was there, outside the toilet block at the corner of Parker's Piece. He was preaching again, preaching to no one, preaching only for God.

The weirdest sensation came over me then. Blood rushed in my ears, and my vision wavered. I stopped in my tracks and dug my fingernails into my palms. I would have turned back had Peter not spotted me. He fell silent, awaiting my arrival.

I breathed deeply and walked the last few steps.

When I was close enough, Peter said, 'Please, tell me you read it.'

I nodded.

'From start to finish?'

'Not yet,' I said. 'But I already have a copy. I can give you back yours.'

'What did you make of it?'

I opened my mouth, but nothing came out.

Peter smiled. 'Yes, that was rather a large question. Come, sit with me. Let us talk.'

He gestured towards a bench a few metres into Parker's Piece, just inside the line of trees. It was pitch black over there.

I hesitated.

Peter picked up on this instantly. 'I'm sorry, I didn't think. There's a pub over there. We can sit outside and talk. It's safe. There will be people around.'

I glanced across at the Hog's Head. Yes, there would be others there, but there might also be my father.

'No,' I said. 'Here's fine.'

And I followed Peter into the dark.

* * *

I sat without wiping the bench. My trousers soaked up the moisture. Peter was clearly more accustomed to survival outdoors and spent some time wiping his side of the bench dry. He sat carefully and placed two books on his lap. The first was the Bible he had lent me; the second was a brown, leather-clad tome that bore no identifying markings. He covered them both with a plastic carrier bag to protect them from droplets that dislodged from the branches above.

'Tell me, Nick,' he said once we were settled, 'have you ever spoken with Christ?'

'What do you mean?' I asked.

'Do you pray?' he said. 'Have you ever prayed?'

'I used to.'

'Why did you stop?'

I considered this for a few moments. When I was younger, I would pray every night after cleaning my teeth and putting on my pyjamas. I would kneel at the foot of my bed, close my eyes and press my palms together. How had I slipped out of that routine? Maybe I had been too tired one night and had just skipped it and fallen asleep. The next night, I might have been busy finishing reading a book. After that, well, it must have been easy.

I also recalled stopping shortly after my grandfather was admitted to hospital. That's when we stopped going to church and instead spent our time charting his decline to death.

'No one seemed to be listening,' I said.

'He does listen,' Peter said. 'He knows our every thought, word and deed. And he does reply. You must be able to cast aside all the other noise. Push down your thoughts. You must be ready to listen.'

I had never been able to understand this whole talking with God thing. How did God respond? Was it like a voice in your head, or was it just a feeling? Did he respond in actions, in coincidences, in the temperature of the air and the colour of the sky?

'How does he talk to you?' I asked.

'He talks to me as you talk to me. He is as real to me as you are.'

What was this, some kind of hallucination? How could that be? Peter wasn't alone in his delusion. Across the world, people could describe similar experiences. Was it mass hysteria or a collective recognition of truth?

Peter took out his brown book, opened it up and, to my surprise, tore out a page. It was plain, apart from lines and a margin. He ensured that the book was safely covered by the plastic bag before folding the sheet into quarters. From the folds in his coat, he produced a pencil.

In the first quarter, he drew a circle, on top of that a stick man, and above that the word 'God'.

'This is how the Lord created the universe,' Peter explained. 'Man is the servant on Earth, and God is his Lord.'

He turned to the next section, where he drew another stickman on a globe, but the word 'God' was erased this time.

'This is how the unenlightened live their lives.' He gave the stickman a misshapen crown. 'Man has become his own king. The only problem is that he does not know what he is doing. When his affairs lose their order, all that man sees above him is the night sky, the fires of countless dying stars. God is still there, but we cannot see Him; we have turned away from Him and believe we are alone. Nobody can hope to survive like this. Man has disrupted the world's equilibrium and feels empty inside. If you ever feel that things just aren't right, that you're not living your life as you should, this is why.'

Peter turned to the third quarter, where Christ entered the equation.

'Jesus Christ died to offer us a second chance. If we accept His forgiveness and honour him as our Lord, we can return to living as we should. There is no need to search inside ourselves for a reason: we can talk to Christ and let Him guide us. He is our Lord, and we are His instruments.'

With that, Peter completed the fourth picture. Christ was placed above man and Earth.

And Peter had me. He had drawn me in.

'This is what I want you to do,' he said, safe in the knowledge that I would obey. 'I want you to pray to God with all your being, pray for guidance, pray for forgiveness for your sins. I want you to think hard about everything we say today. And I want you to read the Good Book. Christ is the way in. His teachings and His sacrifice make the way clear.'

Peter spoke with such authority that I had little choice. He was a great teacher despite his appearance. As we talked further, the man who emerged from the dark had greater depth than the preacher I had seen in the street. Peter understood much and seemed able to empathise with exactly where I was coming from, as though he had been there himself. And I could believe it, too. His body was ragged with experience.

Even so, we didn't discuss anything about my life. Peter only wanted to talk about Christ. Somehow, everything we discussed about this man who lived two thousand years ago seemed relevant to me.

Peter was prone to read certain sections of the Bible in a

great intoning voice, but his voice softened when he turned to the life of Christ. He asked questions to ensure I followed, listened patiently to my interpretations, and never once dismissed my ideas, just modified them. He didn't keep me there too long, either. As soon as he recognised that I was getting tired, he closed the Bible. He left me needing more.

This was to be the first of many sessions.

# Chapter 7

## *Family*

I should take a moment here to make a disclaimer.

Religion is a touchy subject; I'm well aware of that. Had there never been any differences in opinion about matters of faith, humankind's history would be blemished by a lot fewer wars, beheadings, burnings, stonings, drownings, bombings, stabbings and other general unpleasantness. So, let me be clear that I write here only about my experience with religion, specifically Christianity. My journey with Christianity was, to put it mildly, rather unusual. I'm in no position to judge the faith in general or anybody else's beliefs other than mine. And maybe Peter's. But that's for later.

The next day, I dug out my copy of the New Testament. It was at the bottom of my wardrobe, with old school textbooks layered with dust. I sneezed for five minutes after uncovering it. Mum called 'bless you' up the stairs so often that I became more irritated with her than the sneezing itself.

I was reading from it when the phone rang. It was late, and Mum was downstairs eating dinner, so I left it for her to answer. It was a fair bet, anyway, that it was one of her friends calling for a heart-to-heart. That's what occupied the phone line after 9 p.m.

I was so astonished when Mum called my name up the stairs that I waited for her to call it twice.

'Brian for you,' she said when I got to the landing.

I ran down and grabbed the handset.

Brian got straight to the point. 'I just wanted to check you're still coming tomorrow.'

'Where?'

'The trials. You said you'd come and support Adam.'

'Did I?'

'You will be there, won't you?' Brian's tone indicated he wouldn't take 'no' for an answer.

So that was my Saturday booked up.

Mum pouted exaggeratedly when I told her. 'I was hoping we could spend some time together this weekend.'

'Sorry.' It was the best I could manage.

'Do you need a lift?' Mum asked. 'I can drive you if you like.'

'No thanks. I'm going with Brian.'

'What about money?' Mum reached for her purse. 'You'll want to get yourself something nice to eat.'

'I'm fine.'

'Oh.'

What was going on? Until then, Mum had seemed content enough to leave me to my own devices. Now, she seemed to want to stake a claim to my weekend.

I headed back up the stairs, then paused halfway up. Even as a teenager, I wasn't a complete bastard.

'How about Sunday?'

Mum smiled. 'It's a date.'

* * *

'It's nice to have you over. Brian's always pleased to see you.'

'Thanks, Mrs Conrad,' I said.

'Oh Nick, you don't have to call me that! Do I address you as Master Farlowe? No, you *must* call me Sheila.'

I smiled politely, and Mrs Conrad ushered me into the living room, pausing to instruct me to remove my shoes. She directed me to sit on a luxurious-looking armchair before dashing off to get tea and biscuits. Brian had chores to complete before he could come down.

I had only met Brian's mum once before, when I bumped into him and his family at a summer fete. The over-riding impression I'd got was that she was loud. I'm not just referring to the volume of her voice, but more her overall bearing. Some people just have a lot to say. They breeze here and there, setting off little whirlwinds of activity.

Mrs Conrad returned with a tray and placed it on the coffee table. She had brought in a couple of teacups, a plate of biscuits and a little teapot, which looked comical in its thick tea cosy. Apparently, I was to be entertained while we waited for Brian.

'You must excuse me,' she said, following my gaze. 'I'm afraid we only have Earl Grey.'

'That's quite all right,' I replied in my poshest voice.

Mrs Conrad poured the tea, and I did my best to continue the charade that I was practised at this sort of thing. I picked up my cup, gripping it with only my thumb and index finger, and extending my little finger at a right angle. I took the daintiest of sips.

'It's a nice place you've got here,' I said because I felt obliged to.

'Thank you,' said Mrs Conrad, sweeping her arm

expansively to take in the whole living room. 'Our humble abode.'

The place was immaculate, with expensive-looking wallpaper and unsullied deep-pile carpets. Every surface was polished to perfection. There were new-age trinkets everywhere: hoards of crystals, slabs of amethyst, and decorative ashtrays made from giant seashells. It matched Mrs Conrad to a tee. She wore a tartan jacket, well cut, with a butterfly pendant on one of the lapels. Her neck was laden with pearls and charms, all so precisely arranged that you could have measured the symmetry with a mirror. Her make-up must have taken hours to apply. It was as though she had conjured eyes, eyebrows, cheeks and lips from nothing at all.

I felt a million miles away from Peter and his Christ.

Mrs Conrad proceeded to relate the lengthy history of the building's renovation. I listened and nodded in the appropriate places but had pretty much switched off to what she was saying. Every now and then, between nods, I glanced into the hallway, hoping to catch sight of Brian. I could hear a vacuum cleaner going somewhere upstairs and the occasional bang as it impacted walls and furniture. He must have been hurrying.

Eventually, just as Mrs Conrad was getting around to telling me about their plans for a conservatory, Brian appeared in the doorway.

'Shall we go?'

I jumped up. 'Yes.'

Mrs Conrad glanced at the antique clock on the mantelpiece. 'Just in time. You almost made us late, Brian. Go and get your sister, and we'll be off.'

Mrs Conrad had dropped Adam off at the pool earlier, so there was just her, me, Brian and his sister in the car. We parked in the multi-storey right next to Fenners. Brian informed me of the reason for this extreme laziness: we were conserving our energy for the competition.

It was amazing how quiet the place was. I had only ever been there when it was packed. We were the first people in the stalls. The pool was empty.

Mrs Conrad picked us seats in the front row. She placed her handbag on her lap and perched there, still as a statue. I got stuck between her and Brian's sister, who was too engrossed in *Bridget Jones' Diary* to acknowledge me. I couldn't speak to Brian. We just sat there and waited for Adam to make an appearance.

By then, four or five rows had filled up with an elite corps of loyal supporters. When the races started, everyone leapt to their feet and started yelling like lunatics. I did the same. I got quite into it, actually. The excitement was intoxicating. Adrenaline surged through my veins, and I could understand why people live their lives by sport. I experienced almost every emotion as those bodies wriggled and splashed from one end of the pool to the other. I felt a kinship with Brian and his family. We all wanted the same thing. Every one of us was bellowed, 'Come on, Adam!' at the top of our lungs. His sister even put her book away.

It was a shame that I was supporting the wrong swimmer. I had somehow convinced myself that Adam was in lane four when he was actually in three. In my defence, it's practically impossible to distinguish between people wearing swimming caps doing the front crawl. My guy won, and Adam, well, he didn't. When I turned to high-five Brian to celebrate victory, he was holding his head in his hands.

That sobered my mood. By the time Brian's mum dropped me home, I had retreated into my usual world.

* * *

Not everything about my family was bad. For example, I would have run away from home if Mrs Conrad were my mother. One positive thing about my parents and I was that we were kind of singing from the same hymnbook – we might disagree about a word or two here and there, maybe even about an entire verse, but overall, we could relate to each other. Perhaps that's natural; maybe it results from being brought up by them; maybe if I'd been brought up a Conrad, I'd have ended up another Brian. That doesn't bear thinking about.

I have warm memories of the holidays we went on as a family. My parents were always keen on going up to Scotland. I'm not sure why: we had no friends or relatives up there. It was just a tolerable holiday destination that fell within my parents' budget. The cottage we rented, always the same one tucked away in the sunny climes of the highlands, became a second home to me. Returning south, I missed its scummy 'natural spring' swimming pool and the parched conservatory with its flaking paint.

A whole lifetime of experience got crammed into those weeks. There was the nine-hour drive, with its traffic jams, overheating engines, toilet breaks left so late it was painful and, of course, the Beatles' *White Album*, which my father insisted on playing again and again so many times that I gained some empathy with the man who shot Lennon. There was the unpacking, shoving socks into empty drawers, and stocking the kitchen. The first thing I always did was check that the toilet flushed properly. If there was a problem, it was best to find out sooner rather than later. We explored, we argued, and we bought each other ice creams. Sometimes, I met new friends and spent half the time trying to understand what they were saying.

I could never quite penetrate the Scottish accent, but I worked to the rule of thumb that they spent most of the time complaining about the English. It served me well.

I dated my life by those holidays. It was they that aged me.

Each year, it came as a surprise to return home to find everything exactly the same as before. I hadn't expected Cambridge, as a city, to change – with the university at its centre, it seems stuck in the Renaissance – but I had hoped for more from its inhabitants. Still, the same girl worked the express checkout at Sainsbury's. Her skin was spray-tanned all year round. And my friends, well, there was never any need to ask them what they had been up to – wargaming or watching reruns of *Star Trek*. They rarely ventured outside and remained as pale as ever.

It was like we, as a family, had shared something that no one else could touch. Those holidays, those shared experiences, made us a unit. Maybe that's why I felt so distant from my mother in those last months of the millennium. She didn't know what I was doing after school. She had no idea what I was reading and the concepts I tackled upstairs, in my little room.

That afternoon, after getting back from the pool, I lay back on my bed and read the Bible. I was really getting into it by that point. The sun went down, and grey turned to black. I switched on the bedside lamp and continued to read.

Mum came in at about six o'clock. She knocked but didn't wait for an answer. By this time, my muscles had lain pretty much dormant for hours, so I wasn't too quick to tuck my Bible under the covers. All Mum saw was me hiding something away and looking sheepish. She did a double-take but didn't ask any questions.

'Dinner's ready,' she said before backing away.

I went down and ate with her. Then, I went back up to my room and continued to read. I didn't turn my light out until well after midnight.

I woke on Sunday morning to the clang of pans downstairs. It was around half-nine. Soon afterwards, the front door creaked open before being pushed closed. Mum was being careful not to wake me.

I drifted in and out of sleep until about eleven, when I forced myself to get up. It was about then that I heard the garage door open. To me, this was significant and warranted investigation. The garage and shed were strictly my father's domain.

I slipped on some tracksuit bottoms and a loose T-shirt. I pulled back the curtains and looked down at the street. My father's car wasn't outside, but I could see the bonnet of Mum's in the drive. It must have been her pottering about in the garage, reclaiming a part of the house that had always been denied her.

When I went downstairs, I discovered that Mum had made breakfast for us. It was a full, proper meal. I caught a whiff of sizzling bacon from halfway down the stairs. It was the most wonderful smell. The kitchen table was set, with a wipe-clean chequered cloth pulled across it. There were grapefruit halves, orange juice, cereal, croissants and racks stuffed full of toast. Mum was standing by the hob, prodding the contents of a frying pan with a spatula. Her apron was spattered with grease.

We hadn't eaten a breakfast like that in years. My grandparents on my father's side always used to cook fry-ups. They fried haggis, black pudding and Mars bars. They lived in Devon, so we didn't visit them often. For the first few days, whenever we got back, Mum would put us on a diet comprising mainly of lettuce.

Anyway, full English breakfasts conjure in me recollections of happier days when everyone got up at the same time to face the day together.

'There you are!' Mum said. 'I was about to come and wake you up. Better get tucked in.'

I pulled up a chair and grabbed a couple of slices of toast. My mouth was watering like anything.

It was then that things started to go wrong. The toast had clearly been burnt. It was paper-thin from being scraped, and it had an awful carbon taste to it. I tried smothering it with marmalade, but it didn't help.

It got worse when Mum brought over the rest of the food. The scrambled eggs were crispy with sculptures of crystallised fat, the sausages were still frozen in the middle, and little pebbles sat in place of beans. I fought the urge to push my plate to one side in disgust.

'You're thinking about him, aren't you?' Mum said as I munched my way valiantly through the meal.

I had been staring absent-mindedly at the empty chair at the head of the table. Mum had hung her apron over it when sitting down. I hadn't actually been thinking about my father. I had merely noted that there were only two of us at the table.

'He doesn't deserve it,' Mum told me.

I looked up at her, and the illusion of a happy family breakfast shattered utterly. Mum's face was drawn in black and white. The skin beneath her eyes was stained with purple capillaries.

'How long have you hated him?' I asked and regretted it

instantly. It came out completely wrong. I'm not sure what I was trying to say, but it wasn't that.

Mum gave me a cold stare, the likes of which I hadn't seen in over a decade. 'That's how you see it, is it? I did everything I could to make sure you had parents, and I did it because I love you. But there's only so much I can take. I didn't know you wanted me to stay with him until he broke me. I'd have done it without question if you'd have asked me to. He's an evil, spiteful man, and he doesn't deserve to have anything to do with you.'

We passed the rest of the meal in silence. I knew it was up to me to apologise, but I couldn't find the words.

When we finished eating, Mum scraped our plates and deposited them in the sink. I was about to return to my room when she grabbed my hand and led me out of the back door. It was freezing outside, and I had nothing on my feet, but I was too surprised to object.

Mum led me across the garden to the garage, where a brand-new mountain bike was waiting for me, propped up against my father's tool cupboard.

'With your father gone, there's a lot more money floating around,' Mum explained. 'I decided to spend some of it on you.'

I took a couple of tentative steps towards the bike. I didn't know much about bicycles, but this one looked pretty good. It had about twenty gears and suspension built into the frame. The best thing about it was how clean it looked. I didn't dare touch it.

Was it that which made me hesitate or something else?

'I'm allowed to buy a present for my son, aren't I?' Mum said.

I stopped stone dead. Why did this feel so forced?

Unfortunately, my efforts to pinpoint what was wrong just made me sound like a spoilt brat:

'It's winter, Mum. What am I supposed to do with a bike in winter? My fingers will freeze off!'

'I'll buy you some gloves, then.'

'And that makes it all okay, I suppose!'

I knew I was in the wrong, but it was impossible to back down by that point. Her gift was great; it opened up Cambridge for me. No more traipsing around in the dark. But this bike wasn't a true gift. It was political.

I spent the rest of the day in my room. Mum sent me there as punishment for being ungrateful, but I didn't care. I looked to the Bible for help, but it was no good; I couldn't concentrate. My head was a muddle.

Was this anger I was feeling? The more I considered this, the more I worried. Had I inherited this rage from my father? Was his role in the household now mine? Was I growing into it with every minute he was away? For my own good, I had to rid myself of his influence.

I tried to write down how I felt, to expunge it through my pen. The letters I wrote bit into the paper, scarring it forever, but it was like trying to capture a demon in a cage. I couldn't do justice to how I felt with words bolted down one regimented syllable after another. It was more primal than that.

The only thing that worked was violence. I'd like to say I did something spectacular, like trashing the place, in an unfettered display of masculine energy. In truth, I spent the next fifteen minutes snapping every pencil I could lay my hands on. It was deliberate, slow and calculated, and somehow exactly what I needed. As splinters and graphite dust settled on my bedroom carpet, only then did I breathe.

# Chapter 8

## *Holy Man*

I met with Peter a couple of days later, after school. I had to walk there. While Mum hadn't formally withdrawn her gift, its existence was intimately linked with an episode I didn't want to revisit. Looking back, given what Peter and I were about to discuss, it was probably no bad thing that I went there with nothing.

We had arranged to meet on a bench in Midsummer Common, across the river from the boathouses. Peter studied there a lot. This was to become our regular meeting spot and a part of Cambridge that I always now avoid.

I could barely see the boathouses in the half-light. They were just big sheds with insignia attached, all locked up. The wind was strong, so the common was all but deserted. Only the most health-conscious of joggers had ventured out, alongside those dog owners that were most under their pet's thumb (or paw). Most of the barges along the riverbank lay dormant. Those that were occupied spouted steam from quaint pipe chimneys. Their window shutters were closed. The whole city had better things to do than be outside.

When Peter and I had arranged our meeting, it hadn't seemed weird at all, but by then, we had spent quite a bit of time in each other's company. I had got used to him. When I returned, any familiarity had been dampened by the passing of days. I was, let's face it, going to meet a strange man, and I had been brought up with all manner of stories about child abduction. I remembered a film they played me as an infant: *Stranger Danger!* I had been programmed to feel a cramp in my stomach.

The sight of him didn't help. As I approached along the footpath by the river, I could see him in profile. His head was lowered. His white beard engulfed his neck and the lower half of his face. He had pulled a sheet around him, cape-like, but it didn't look like it offered much protection from the cold. Initially, I thought he was asleep, but as I neared, I caught sight of a book in his lap. That image was totally at odds with his surroundings. He was sitting there, scribbling in that book of his with a pencil stub, even as the wind whipped around him and cast dead leaves from trees. Grass flattened in waves, and water droplets were kicked up from the river. Nothing was calm, nothing except Peter. Only his fingers moved, coaxing letters from flaking graphite.

I confess that he frightened me. Not in the straightforward, physical way of my father – I knew where I stood with that – but because Peter was impossible to predict. He never went with convention. Even straightforward rules, such as those that dictated that you sheltered from a storm, didn't seem to apply.

Peter didn't notice me until I was standing right next to him. It wasn't until I leaned over his shoulder to look at what he was writing that he sprang to life, tucking his book into a carrier bag before I could get a decent view.

'Won't you give an old man some privacy?' he said, but his tone was friendly enough. He invited me to sit.

'What are you writing?' I asked.

'My great work,' Peter said. 'Everyone has one story in them, even if it's their own.'

'It's an autobiography, then?'

'Of a sort. Sometimes, the point of writing isn't to tell the story but to allow others to see the world as you see it. Do you understand that, my son?'

I nodded without thinking about it too deeply. I would only come to understand what he meant later.

'Have you continued your studies?' asked Peter.

'I've finished the Gospels now,' I said. 'I'm onto Corinthians.'

'Now, now, let us not go rushing ahead of ourselves. You need to understand the context. Do you realise the enormity of what you've just read? The Lord sent His only son to Earth. God was made flesh, and He died for our sins. Think about that. What does it mean to you?'

'I don't know.'

'It must mean something!'

Okay, this was new. I had read the Gospels before and knew the story of Christ inside out, but nobody had ever asked me to explain what I thought about it.

'It kind of makes me feel like I've got a duty,' I ventured. 'An obligation to live life the way I should. To make sure Christ's sacrifice wasn't for nothing.'

'Good. And what does it mean to live life the way you should?'

I considered this for a moment. 'I don't know, maybe following God's plan. Doing what he wants me to do...'

I faltered. It was patently obvious that I was just telling Peter what he wanted to hear. My mind was elsewhere, preoccupied by something I had read in the New Testament. Christ recruited disciples by instructing them to give away all their belongings and follow him. I remembered this being the subject of one of the more heated sermons I sat through when I was younger. That service had ended with an appeal to raise money for the starving in Africa. It was a powerful message which had filled the collection tin. And it really got to the root of Christianity as I saw it: guilt. Christ's words made me feel bad about wearing clean clothes and new shoes, about eating well and drinking fresh water.

For some reason, all the days I had lived until then seemed unbelievably happy, like cherished home video moments. Most lives aren't all that bad when viewed as snippets. We've all watched terrible films because they've managed to cobble together a decent trailer from the good bits. In the grand scheme of things, my life wasn't too bad at all. It was just going through a wobbly patch, a transition.

Nobody who'd had it as good as me could have contact with the divine. I hadn't suffered enough. I had been sedated by the days, by the simple fact that my parents paid for my meals and put a roof over my head. Was such comfort illusory? Did it exist only on the path to damnation?

But what was the solution? The idea of giving away everything I owned was abhorrent. It's not that I was too greedy to do that; it's more that I recognised that reducing oneself to abject poverty was actually a pretty stupid thing to do. It occurred to me that Peter *was* living as Christ intended. Where else should a true disciple of Christ be but on the street? But was that the only way to save your soul? And, if so, how was the world supposed to function if everybody did it?

As I sat there, guilt flowed through my veins; guilt that I inhabited a healthy body and was born into a middle-class family in a prosperous country. All my possessions and all the possibilities open to me, they all weighed heavy.

'I know I don't live the way I should,' I said, 'but I want to.'

The words hung there.

Peter studied me for a while. He was undoubtedly trying to ascertain how serious I was about this. What he concluded, I don't know. Even I didn't know how seriously to take myself.

Eventually, Peter spoke softly, kindly: 'That is the first step, Nick.'

The next step, he explained, involved seeking out God through prayer and reading the holy texts. Peter instructed me to start praying again every night before getting into bed. At first, I was sceptical, but that night, in my pyjamas, I decided I had nothing to lose. I prayed to be heard and for eternal life for everyone I knew. I couldn't shake the feeling that I was talking to myself, and I didn't know what was scarier – the idea that there was no one out there or that somebody was listening and watching, judging my every move.

Under Peter's influence, the focus of my reading changed. Gradually, I cut down on science fiction and started reading more history and theology. I didn't think of this as a sacrifice: I was still engaged in the same general line of enquiry, still picking worlds apart to see how they worked, but it was my own planet that concerned me now.

'Books are instruments given to us by God to understand Christ's message,' Peter told me once. 'Through them, we can gain the knowledge to save ourselves.'

I'm not sure I approached it precisely as he intended,

though. Undoubtedly, Peter hoped that this reading would trigger some kind of revelation. He kept talking about taking a 'leap of faith', but I teetered on the edge of the abyss, unwilling to take the plunge until I knew how deep it dropped. I buried myself in the technical elements: doctrinal disputes, Aryanism, iconoclasm, and transubstantiation. Any conversion I underwent had to be a decision informed by knowledge. Christianity had to make sense to me; there had to be a clear equation that led logically to God.

I soon outgrew the public library and found myself turning to some of the less accessible Cambridge institutions. Infiltrating the college libraries, now that was a challenge. I was only a few years off university age, but we change a lot in our teens. I had to masquerade as some kind of prodigy, sent off early to study in the colleges' hallowed walls. I learnt quickly that the key to infiltration is confidence. We walk differently when we know we're trespassing. My first attempts to get past the college porters saw me walking around with my shoulders hunched, taking slow, twitchy steps while desperate to run and hide somewhere before I got spotted. I was politely but firmly asked to leave. Then I watched this one guy who clearly wasn't a member of college (he didn't have a posh enough voice) breeze past a porters' lodge with only a brief nod to one of the bowler-hatters. Following his example, I started walking like I stepped the same flagstones daily and found my surroundings – those pristine lawns and buildings steeped with history – wholly unremarkable. I wasn't challenged again.

Of the diverse things I read, one resonated with me in particular. I'll mention it now as it helps explain why I pursued this obsession. I learned about the role of the holy man in early Christianity. Across the Roman Empire, pious men and women took up residence in caves or exiled themselves to the desert to battle Satan's servants. They faced temptation on a daily basis, and they survived through the power of the Holy Spirit, even as their bodies withered away. These holy men and women forsook the shells they lived in, for flesh was the plaything of the Devil, who lured souls into damnation and manipulated the weak with worldly desires.

As I sat poring over the accounts of these saints' lives, the centuries between their lifetimes and mine dissolved to nothing. I could picture the stylites atop their pillars just outside the library window. I would see their weathered bodies outlined against the sunset, their arms outstretched as they fended off the demons that plagued them. Finally, their strength would give way, and they would topple to the ground like discarded hand puppets.

It's only possible to believe these things happened if you put human faces to the characters. It's people we believe in, not dry facts. People make history something more than a textbook. There's an immediacy to them, a humanity that gives the past relevance today. If you can believe in a person, their world comes with them: the events they lived through, the miracles they witnessed, the lessons they learnt. Religion implants itself in reality.

Even back then, these holy people had a similar effect. The textbooks tell of Christianity eradicating paganism, but this wasn't straightforward. Coming from paganism, people were accustomed to divine entities that at least took an interest in their affairs. The Christian god was unapproachable, barricaded behind the institutions of the church. It was the holy man that offered this point of continuity. His blessing could save a crop or pull a child out of a coma, and it could purchase everlasting life for a dying soul.

People needed holy men. It was they who made Christianity real.

At sixteen, I felt that same need. I had started thinking about death a lot. You might think I was too young for that, with the whole of my life ahead of me, but it accompanied the realisation that structures I had thought were there to stay could crumble to nothing. I had never thought our family was perfect, but I hadn't conceived that it could be so fragile. This change impressed upon me that all things must pass; it made death real.

Christianity offered comfort. Follow Christ, and I would have eternal life. He loved me unconditionally, and he would *always* be there.

And the proof of his existence: Peter.

* * *

I met with Peter every few days. When I wasn't with him, I spent the early evening in the library. The rest of my life faded to insignificance. The days passed without incident, always as expected. I woke up in an empty house, went downstairs in my dressing gown, and ate cereal. Then I dressed, made my lunch and went to school, where I copied down notes mechanically, barely registering more than the sound of the teachers' words. I lost at chess, had my fair share of awkward moments with Jo, and was treated to a tutorial from Brian about the 'Bishop's Gambit'.

During P.E. lessons, which I skipped due to my heart condition, I plodded my way through *I Am Legend*, a paranoid sci-fi vampire thriller by Richard Matheson. This was my one concession to past tastes. However, my enjoyment of this novel was severely impeded by vivid memories of the film they based on it. *Omega Man*, it was called, and

Michael had made me watch it a few months earlier. It starred Charlton Heston and featured vampires wearing terrible 70s sunglasses – those huge round ones that cover half the face. Creatures of the night that made such a severe fashion mistake had no business being frightening (or immortal, for that matter).

Science fiction wasn't as serious an issue for me as before.

I found everything exhausting, but my mind wouldn't let me sleep. It was always racing this way and that, yapping like an overexcited puppy when I tried to quieten it at night. During the daytime, I faced the opposite problem. I couldn't get it to budge. Somewhere along the way, it had turned nocturnal.

One evening, I was home alone because the library was closed. I didn't answer the phone, even though it rang several times. I just sat in the front room as the sky darkened and everything turned orange. It was silent, and everything felt soft and subdued. I was content just sitting there, with nothing and no one intruding on that time and space of mine. I felt like I should have been praying but couldn't persuade myself to get to my knees.

It was almost nine o'clock when Mum came in. I felt like I hadn't spoken to her in forever. In truth, I probably hadn't, unless you count the occasional 'yes' or 'no', 'hello' or 'goodbye'.

'Are you in, Nick?' she called after closing the front door and turning on the hall light.

'Yes.'

'I brought home Chinese. Are you hungry?'

'I've already eaten.' I had nibbled at a frozen pizza, cremated by a few minutes in the microwave.

'Where are you?' Mum said.

I could see her in the hallway, looking upstairs for light from my bedroom. I hadn't been up there at all since getting back from school. I was still wearing my coat.

'I'm in here,' I said.

She peered through the doorway into the living room.

'What are you doing sitting in the dark?'

'Sometimes...' I began, but I trailed off.

I wanted to tell her that I found it easier to focus in the dark, where I could dwell on every passing second. Everything appeared more immediate, and life in general seemed that much sadder. In the dark, I could open myself up. When I listened to my favourite songs, I really *felt* them, like there was just me and this singer and this wealth of emotion, alone in infinity.

Instead of saying any of this, I turned to a subject that I hadn't mentioned in a while:

'Have you heard from Dad yet?'

It occurred to me that, at some point, I had stopped wondering if my father would come back. I wasn't sure what had prompted that and whether it was a good or bad thing.

But Mum had already disappeared into the kitchen to get dinner ready. After a few moments, I pushed myself out of the armchair and went to join her.

# Chapter 9

## *The Life of Brian*

It started one lunchtime. Or, at least, that's when I first noticed it.

Chess club was cancelled because Mr Finn was off sick. All the regular attendees got turfed onto the playground with the rest of the riffraff. I wasn't used to being around so many people. Several first-years were playing tag (or 'it', or whatever you might call it – someone should do a regional study). One of them bumped into me before disturbing the fourth-years' football game. All I could do was stand there, dazed. A group of second-years were trying to play ultimate frisbee on the school field, but this had to be abandoned because of the wind. Everybody was milling around, and I didn't have anyone to talk to.

I had to hold out until half twelve, when I would meet Sam and Michael outside the dinner hall. They both ate hot dinners and never usually attended chess club, so this was the first lunch I would spend with them in a while. It was a shame that lunch hour would be half over by the time they finished.

I staked a claim to a spot on the wall outside the dinner

hall and ate my sandwiches while looking across the staff car park. A chicken-wire fence separated this area from the playing field, but it wasn't very high. In the past, the occasional stray ball had found its way over. This was always costly. A teacher, Mrs Ennis, patrolled the car park, hawk-eyed, jingling the keys to her BMW. Many theories were working their way around school about how Mrs Ennis could afford a BMW on a teacher's salary. I favoured the mundane explanation of a rich husband, but Sam was convinced that she had an illicit trade in exam answer sheets.

I liked watching people, picking out patterns of behaviour, bearing witness to people losing their individuality as they moved with the crowd. It was comforting fading into the background and taking on the role of the observer, forgetting that I, too, was one of those helpless, predictable creatures. Anyone who's sat by the window in a high street café will know what I mean: there are only so many things people can do when walking down the street. Watch them long enough, and you will find repetition. Life loses its random element, and you end up almost able to see its cogs turning.

As I sat there that day, the flurry of movement that initially overloaded my senses gradually lost the illusion of chaos and started to solve itself like a quadratic equation. Peter talked to me once about God's order, about how everything can be explained with reference to Him. According to Peter, God was the single unifying principle behind all human endeavour. I found it easier to believe that life could be so simplified, watching the school playground turn into the Serengeti. Kids followed teachers around, begging for favours like scavengers craving scraps of meat. Girls moved in pairs, playing at being best friends. Most of the rest moved as herds, seeking safety and encouragement in numbers. Then there were the individuals...

Brian was in a world of his own when he entered the panorama. I could tell it was him from a distance because he was the only one in school who still had a full-on proper lunchbox, a bright red affair, a relic from his primary school years (I think it bore a *Power Rangers* sticker back then, but it had long since peeled off). He seemed to be in a world of his own. I have no idea what he was thinking about, but it affected how he walked. He kept his knees locked so his legs stayed straight as he paced, making him sway from side to side like he was on stilts. I spotted this from right across the car park. Other kids were nearer. There was never any doubt that they would notice him.

A group of six or seven kids converged on Brian as he walked by. They were casual about what they did next, a knack that only came from practice. It seemed almost accidental when one of them knocked Brian's lunchbox out of his hands. His beaker of squash was the first to hit the ground, splitting and darkening the cement. Then food became litter: his apple bruised, cling film muddied, and crisps got trampled into the ground. Brian being Brian, the pack also contained three chocolate bars and a spicy sausage (the potency of which explained why no one wanted to sit next to him in class after lunch), but their wrappers spared them from contamination.

I recognised faces and backs of heads as the mob surrounded him. None were in our year – they were all younger than us. Brian's age made him a trophy to them.

They pushed him, really pushed him. It would have been impossible for anyone to keep his balance, and Brian was – how can I put it – rather heavily built, so once they'd got him moving, he had a lot of momentum to fight against.

He bounced from one side to the other of the loose circle of bodies that formed around him. They pushed him again and again. He stumbled this way and that, whirling and flailing, struggling to stay on his feet. They were chanting and shouting in his face. I was too far away to make out what they were saying, but their tone was intimidating.

I set my lunch to one side and stood, knowing it was up to me to do something to stop it. I looked for the teacher, but she was on the other side of the car park, busy reprimanding a pair of lads who had been demonstrating their lack of hand-eye coordination with a cricket ball. I looked back at Brian, who had resigned himself to being shunted like a pinball. His legs were bowed now, and his head hung loose.

I couldn't move. It was inertia as much as anything. Analysing it, there were probably two other considerations. First, I didn't think it would assist Brian's cause if I went over there. It would only set a precedent, and he had to fight his own battles. The second reason, sadly, was that no one in that group had ever bothered me, and I was in no hurry to change that. Besides, it was almost over. They would leave him alone soon.

Every second that passed was agony. I desperately wanted to emulate the heroes I watched on television and leap to Brian's aid, but I couldn't. I was totally inadequate. Worse than that, I was going through the same ordeal as Brian. I've read somewhere that the root of empathy lies in the brain's ability to simulate whatever emotion we witness. You see someone laugh, and you smile instinctively, and if someone starts getting funny with you (however justified they might be), you get angry, too. They were barging into Brian now, and I could almost feel their shoulders in my stomach, knocking the wind out of me.

Finally, they let him go. Someone in the group stepped

aside just as Brian was tumbling towards him. Brian must have been so disoriented that he didn't realise he was about to collide with a wall. I looked away.

When I turned back, the gang was parading past Brian, member by member, spitting out closing insults. In a perverted way, they looked like funeral mourners, taking their time to file past an open coffin.

By the time I got there, they had dispersed.

I picked up Brian's lunchbox. A few fresh scrape marks accompanied the existing ruts. Brian had rolled himself over and sat with his back propped against the wall. His head was tilted back, his mouth wide, taking deep breaths. There was a nasty gash on his forehead, and his palms were grazed from where he had tried to break his fall at the last minute.

I held a hand out to him, offering to help him up. Brian just looked away.

I squatted down so that I was at his level. He still didn't say anything.

Eventually, I took it upon myself to make a suggestion:

'You should tell a teacher.'

Brian studied me. 'That's what you think, is it? I should just go running to a 'grownup', and they'll sort it out. What exactly do you think they'd do?'

'They'd have a word with them,' I replied. 'Bullies aren't brave. They won't do anything if they know someone has their eye on them.'

'You don't have a clue.' Brian got up and grabbed his lunchbox off me. 'I'm going to get cleaned up. Please don't follow me.'

He turned his back on me and walked off. I attempted to follow him into the school building, but he slammed the door in my face. I didn't need further hints that he wanted to be left alone.

When I think back to my childhood, it is places I remember more than events. I recognise buildings and landscapes, although sometimes I can't think why. Car parks, sports halls, restaurants and village greens; my world takes its character from the activity it witnessed.

I find it impossible to visit zoos these days without thinking about my father. Glass cages and weather-beaten picnic tables have assumed significance from the presence of my dysfunctional family, and painful twinges of familiarity are all I have in place of memories.

My mind's eye has a clearer view when it comes to that corner of the school beside the staff car park. I can't even picture it without reliving that attack on Brian. It's painfully vivid. Many parts of my account so far have been based on vague recollections. It has sometimes proven impossible to remember how someone phrased a sentence or the exact order of events that took place years ago. I had no problem with this particular episode. I just strolled into the school grounds one Saturday and sat on that wall outside the dining hall. All the debris that had found its way into my brain since then dropped away, and I was back there, eating my lunch as my friend was getting the crap kicked out of him. I could have sworn I caught a whiff of canteen lasagne and undercooked potatoes from the dormant school kitchen, clear as memory.

I was as useless to sixteen-year-old Brian then as I am now. I was so wrapped up in myself that I didn't even try to help him. I prayed that night for forgiveness. I think that was the first time I truly believed in humankind's weakness, and that sin might taint us all.

It was not to be the last.

* * *

'That's just how it works,' Sam said when I met him and Michael outside the dinner hall, as planned. 'Brian's a natural victim. It's human nature to pick on anyone who stands out from the crowd, and Brian, well, he's different.'

Sam considered himself a great student of human nature. He was prone to waffle on about Jung, Freud and Durkheim, always in a general kind of way. He had a way of making you think he knew more than he actually did.

'That's not particularly helpful,' I said.

Sam grinned as though I had just said the most ridiculous thing ever. 'What do you want, exactly? Practical advice?'

'Well, *some* kind of advice would be good.'

'Okay, how about this: don't be different. Simple as that. Oh, and if you are different and can't do anything about it, never let anyone else know. People are ignorant. They're afraid of what they don't understand. You just have to accept that.'

I turned to Michael. 'What about you?'

Michael rubbed the back of his neck and glanced up at the sky. The air was so full of tiny water droplets that we had barely noticed our clothes getting soaked. Michael's shirt clung to his skeletal body, and his nipples showed prominent, as though concealed only by tracing paper.

'I've no idea what we ought to do, Nick,' he said. 'I've never been through anything like that before.'

'That's because you're normal,' Sam said.

'Do you know, that's probably the nicest thing you've ever said to me. But is normality a blessing or a curse? Would Bowie have got anywhere if he hadn't stood out? No, he had to become an androgynous alien before he got noticed.'

'Yeah, I find myself pondering that every now and then,' Sam said.

Michael had regained some of his personality in the wake of the 'Tess affair' (as the rest of us lovingly termed it). She had drowned him, if I'm honest. Under her influence, he had become the sensible one who told us if we were being stupid or out of order. I had missed his random comments. I would take a Bowie analogy over one of Sam's rants any day of the week.

It was good, too, to hear Michael talk about somebody other than Tess. A few weeks had passed since they'd stopped seeing each other. The first days had been the hardest. Heartbroken, he had talked about her in hushed tones as though she was a flower so delicate that a light sniff of its scent could tear off petals and destroy it. Gradually, this had changed. His comments had turned icy, and he had started going to ridiculous lengths to avoid her. Only recently had he stopped mentioning her altogether. For months, Michael had been 'the one with the girlfriend'. Now, I was rediscovering who he really was.

'Bullying's just a part of growing up, Nick,' Sam assured me. 'Everybody has to work their own way through these things. They're what toughens us. If you can't cope with it, there's no way you'll be ready for adult life.'

* * *

It happened again later that week. Mr Finn was still off sick, so there was no chess club. Rumours were floating around that he was suffering from all manner of contagious diseases, ranging from syphilis (which one account told of him contracting during a summer holiday break in Amsterdam) through botulism to the black death. The latter theory had been concocted by the first-years, who were getting to grips with the nastier parts of history: first the plague and then, once broken in, the Holocaust.

Brian did his bit to avoid a repeat of the previous episode by securing himself a library pass so he was safe for lunchtime. Instead, they ambushed him in the corridor by his locker after the last lesson. It was a group of boys who'd been hanging around eating crisps, looking menacing and eyeing up girls in my year. When they saw Brian come through the double doors, they made right for him, spreading out shoulder to shoulder to form an impenetrable barrier. They had reached marching speed by the time they got to him, and their pace didn't dip as they barged him face-first into a wall.

It was over as quickly as it had begun, and compared to the previous incident, it was relatively minor. The problem was that such episodes were unremitting. Brian was a natural victim. He must have felt like the whole of the school was against him. Nobody ever passed up the chance to kick him while he was down. I'm sure he was losing weight (not that this was necessarily a bad thing); he was undoubtedly jumpier than before. I learnt quickly that it was a bad idea to come up behind him and pat him on the shoulder.

It happened once when Jo was chatting with me. If ever I felt like I should have done something, it was then. I couldn't believe I was standing there while my friend was being pushed around. Jo didn't comment. She kept on talking. I followed her lead.

What could I do? Bullying was part of the culture – everyone was involved or implicated in some way – and it was routine, just one of those things that happened at break or between lessons. How can you combat that? So much of what happened could have been explained away as accidental, and it was always over by the time I had urged my muscles into action. I'm going to employ precisely the same excuse now that I used to justify why I did nothing about my parents' fights: it seemed inappropriate to bring that kind of thing up after the fact. Is this a common phenomenon with violence? Is there something about its immediacy that gets lost in analysis?

I turned reluctantly to Peter for guidance. I say 'reluctantly' because I had a feeling it wouldn't get me anywhere. As I've mentioned before, he wasn't someone I could imagine talking to about anything but Christianity. Try to engage him in conversation about anything, and he would find a way of slipping God in. Peter always saw the bigger picture. Faith had made him turn his back on comforts like food, warmth and friendship. What possible interest could he have in my affairs?

But who else did I have to turn to?

'It is a difficult situation,' Peter said after listening with remarkable patience as I offloaded. 'You believe that you should act to defend your friend. You think of this as your duty to him.'

Finally, someone who understood!

'But I tell you that your eyes are not clear,' Peter continued. 'You see only what Satan wants you to see. Violence should not beget violence. That is not the way, my son.'

'But you should have been there!' I said. 'You'd know what I'm talking about if you'd have seen it. You've got to fight back. It's the only thing that registers with them. It's all about reputation – you've got to forge it. You can't stop them by just rising above it.'

Peter smiled knowingly. 'I can appreciate why you feel that way. But this matter has been addressed by Our Lord

Jesus Christ Himself. Do you not remember Matthew, chapter five, verses thirty-eight to forty?

'"*Ye have heard that it hath been said, An eye for an eye, and a tooth for a tooth. But I say unto you, that ye resist not evil; but whosoever shall smite thee on thy right cheek, turn to him the other also. And if any man will sue thee at the law, and take away thy coat, let him have thy cloak also.*"'

I laughed. 'I don't think they were after Brian's coat. And if he had a cloak, I'm sure they'd have been welcome to it.'

Peter glared at me. His pupils were pinprick.

I bowed my head. 'I'm sorry.'

Whole hours seemed to pass, with neither of us saying anything. The river flowed past silently. Eventually, Peter shook his annoyance aside and asked me to pray with him. I did so, but my heart wasn't in it. I was still thinking about Brian.

Okay, so neither Brian nor I were allowed to retaliate. Suffer in silence and embrace pain; that was the Lord's way. Great. None of that fitted with life at school. I could see why so many Christians had endured persecution without protest. Whole swathes of history – the actions of thousands of people who died for their faith – could be explained with reference to that passage. When faith refuses to bend to reality, the human body gets broken. That didn't sound too appealing to me.

Still, if I wanted to be a good Christian, no one ever said it would be easy. Love, that was the answer, love of my fellow man. As my brain formulated the idea that evolved from that, I could imagine Sam cackling. If he had found out about this, he would have had ammunition to ridicule me for a decade.

I would be a proper friend.

It was Mum's birthday that Sunday. I had only just remembered about it. I decided it would be a great bonding experience if I asked Brian to help me choose a present.

I hadn't completely lost the plot. I did still realise that only girls enjoy shopping together. 'Enjoy' was the keyword here. We weren't going window shopping or asking each other's opinion of new fashions, and we certainly weren't going to have fun. I hated shopping. I asked Brian along solely for support.

When I cornered him with this proposal, he didn't say anything for a long time. I'm pretty sure he was trying to work out if I was joking. I almost punched the air when he agreed.

Cambridge city centre was harder work than usual that Saturday. It was getting close to Christmas, so the streets were packed with people carrying bagfuls of gifts. To make matters worse, there was no unified direction of traffic. There were too many paths and alleys through town and crossroads where people collided and pushed past each other. It was chaos. And whenever we chanced upon a clear way, someone full of premature festive cheer walked out of a shop without looking and ploughed straight into the two of us.

The older part of town, which contains most of the shops and colleges, was closed to traffic during shopping hours, so we didn't have to worry about getting flattened by delivery lorries. Still, several frustrated cyclists did their best to keep us on our toes.

If getting around was an exhausting experience, I couldn't begin to describe how much energy we expended choosing Mum's present. I relied on Brian a lot when it came to this. He was my eyes and ears. I had lived in

Cambridge all my life, but suddenly, the city centre was alien to me.

Let me explain. I had decided to get Mum some jewellery for the first time. In previous years, I had gone for plain old chocolate, flowers or teddy bears. Dull, I know, but they were a winning formula. This year was different. I felt older, like I should give her something more adult. And since my father was no longer around, Mum wouldn't get her usual necklace or earrings. The problem was that I had no idea where any jewellers were. Those shop fronts only existed on the periphery of my vision, faint twinkles in the corner of eyes that were seeking out *HMV, Waterstones* or *Electronics Boutique.* I had my landmarks – shops that I frequented regularly. The rest didn't matter to me. Until then.

I felt like I was discovering the city again. I couldn't believe how many shops I'd missed. No wonder there were so many people around: there was so much to buy. I kept on the lookout for jewellers, but it was all too much for me. There were too many new things to discover. I walked oblivious past shop windows crammed with precious metals. Brian kept having to call me back. I'm glad he was there. Without him, I'd probably have given up and bought Mum a Gabrielle CD or nipped into *Woolworths* and settled for a 'New Year, 2000' mug and handkerchief set.

Brian was a different person that day. Gone were all those annoying habits I usually associated with him. He was quiet for the most part and comparatively subdued. Everything he said was helpful. He pointed out bargains and deterred me from buying various tacky items that caught my eye. He never once mentioned *Buffy the Vampire Slayer.* Away from his family and our groups of friends, he displayed another side of himself. I used to think he was one-dimensional, that I knew him inside out, but I had to reassess this. I couldn't look down on him anymore or picture him simply as 'the sci-fi nerd'. Where once I had questioned what I had to gain from our friendship, now I was uncertain if I had anything to offer him.

If only others from school could have seen Brian like that. I wondered how they would treat him then. The irony was that he was probably better adjusted than any of them when it came down to it. But that's not the way the world works, I suppose. Brian was Brian, and he was fated to suffer as he did.

# Chapter 10

## *The Fifth Commandment*

Mum told me the news quite bluntly the following morning, ruining what would otherwise have been a pleasant day. The sun was out, the sky was clear, and I had just given her a gold-plated necklace for her birthday. She loved it. She said it was the nicest thing I had ever bought her and went on about how lucky she was to have a son like me. I was inclined to go along with her on both fronts, although I did wish she'd stop saying it.

'By the way,' Mum said, as an afterthought, 'you had better keep next Saturday free.'

I was in the middle of coiling a scarf around my neck when she said this. We were getting ready for church. Mum had decided she wanted to go for her birthday, and I was quite willing to give it another try.

I was never great at multi-tasking, so I stopped and looked at her.

'You're to meet your father,' she explained.

She put on her coat and opened the front door. I continued to look at her.

'It's called a contact meeting,' she explained. 'Both parents have a right to see you.'

'Is that true? I'm sixteen.'

'I'm new to this too, Nick.'

Without another word, she stepped out into the cold. I had little choice but to follow her.

* * *

I fumed all the way through the service, unable to keep still or concentrate on anything the vicar was saying. I tried to follow his sermon, I really did. I locked my eyes on him and focused on his mouth as it conjured wise words, but after a few minutes, I realised I was thinking about something else entirely. It was infuriating because I was eager to listen. And it was all my parents' fault.

All right, so I did harbour some curiosity about my father, but it wasn't ever strong enough to make me want to meet him again. I had been trying to fool myself that all that stuff with him was way in the past and that my religious studies represented a new me, independent of family ties. But no, I was being reeled back in. It had only been a month since my father left. His hold on me was far from broken. The fact that I shared this man's blood translated into an obligation. I would always be bound to him.

When we got back from church, I went straight up to my room, where I spent the rest of the day stewing. I tried to pray, to get some handle on my thoughts again, but it didn't help. I had no pencils left to snap, either. I needed space, but it was freezing outside, and there was no way that Mum would let me out without a firm interrogation.

It was late afternoon by the time I calmed down, after lying on my bed listening to loud music. What was my reward for this triumph of self-control? Homework. With GCSEs on the horizon, I had loads of coursework to get through.

And that was my Sunday.

I wasn't myself when I met with Peter the following night. I avoided company during school, aware that it would take only an unkind word or ill-conceived comment to push me over the edge. I knew that going to see Peter wasn't the best of ideas. He wouldn't understand what I was going through, and even if he did, he'd think it irrelevant. Peter's celibacy, his abstinence, was both physical and emotional. If I was to follow Christ, I had to be calm and measured, and shut off the anger I was feeling. I wasn't strong enough to do that.

But we had arranged to get together, and there was no way I was going to leave him on that bench, waiting for me.

We met in the same place as usual, down by the boathouses. As always, Peter looked like he had been sitting there for hours. He had his Bible open beside him and was busy jotting something in his other book.

Peter looked much healthier that day than any other. His face was fuller – there was something more to it than bone and parchment. His body appeared to have returned from the brink. Immodestly, I wondered how much of that was thanks to me.

We exchanged our 'hellos', and I sat down. We then recited the Lord's Prayer together. This was Peter's way of granting proceedings an official seal. When we were done, he asked me what had happened since our last meeting. Our sessions were routine by then: prayer, then discussion, then Bible reading and analysis, followed by a closing prayer. I should have gone with the flow and told him I'd had an average, boring week. Peter usually had plenty to say, so if I got him on a roll, he might not even realise I was there in body but not in spirit. If I'd have had an ounce of sense, that's how I'd have played it, but I couldn't help myself:

'My Dad used to knock my Mum around,' I said. 'They're separated now. I haven't seen him for weeks. But Mum's told me I've got to go meet him Saturday.'

It came as a relief, saying that, letting it go. It had been eating away at me from the inside, and now it had been released.

Peter drew in breath. I hadn't told him about any of this stuff before. I reckon I could have said what I did to thousands of people, and not one of them would have responded as did Peter:

'Your parents are not godly people,' he said, 'and yet you honour them. You adhere to the fifth commandment, even though it tears you apart.'

'What do you mean they're not godly?'

It was one thing to be pissed off with them and quite another to accept them described in that way.

'Have they taught you as I have? Have they introduced you to the word of God?'

'Well, my Mum took me to church-'

'You came to me a lost soul, shadowed from God's light. When I beheld you, I recognised a good soul cursed by ignorance. At Heaven's gates, ignorance is as fatal as sin. Your parents should have shown you more. They should have introduced you to God's word instead of bickering like children. Look inside your heart, and you will see it is true.'

'Well, they got me this far. It can't have been easy-'

'Stop making excuses for them. I am telling you that you owe them nothing. Did not Our Lord Jesus Christ turn away from his family to pursue his calling? Did He not tell us, "*If any man come to me, and hate not his father, and mother, and wife, and children, and brethren, and sisters, yea, and his own life also, he cannot be my disciple.*" We must be prepared to turn away from everything we love.'

'No,' I said immediately.

Turn away from my parents? Was I honestly ready to do that? Was I supposed to live on the street as Peter did? Was that what he had in mind for me? This was starting to sound ridiculous.

'Why say you 'no'?' asked Peter calmly. 'Do you still cling to the material? Is your reluctance fuelled by ties of flesh and bonds of ownership? Have I taught you no better than that?'

It was then that I finally got it. What was madness to me was reasonable to him. There was no way I could run away from home; I just didn't have it in me. All right, so family life was far from ideal, but it was still at least one step up from homelessness.

It was my fault. I should have realised how Peter would react. His personal faith was one of action. He was so far removed from earthly shackles that he could see no reason for me to stay where I was. We lived in different worlds. Sometimes, it was easy to forget that: we were trying so hard to make his world mine.

Surely, Peter could understand. His life mustn't always have been like that. He must have been young once, with people and possessions that he cherished. He must have thought the same as me at one time. How else could he understand that which he now loathed?

* * *

Peter talked about his life rarely and never with great clarity. His writing gave more detail and structure when I eventually got to read it, but I won't include it here for reasons that will become apparent later. As I write it here, Peter's life is in my own words, filtered through my perceptions. I do this because I feel I need to represent his story, and the best way I can think to do so is to write as him. He wouldn't have wanted it this way. I only hope that, for better or worse, I have done him justice.

As a child, Peter lived with his parents in a caravan – a 'Winchester', two-wheeled, rounded at the top like a well-baked loaf. The walls were made of cream plastic, flimsy as dried twigs from summers in the sun. The floor dipped and creaked under the slightest of weights. Nothing about it seemed built to last.

Peter hated it and never thought of it as home.

His parents were first-generation travellers. They had been on the road since the end of the war. It was shared grief that threw them together: they lost their parents on the same black night, buried beneath twisted iron and conquered masonry in the Blitz-charred remains of their city. This grief had turned into fear, debilitating, the sort that shapes a lifestyle. They shrunk away from all centres of population, associating death with civilisation. Safety lay not in numbers but in solitude. Peter was born into the quivering calm of a storm's aftermath.

Their life was simple. With all their possessions in that mobile home, they could uproot and move on at a moment's notice. Peter's father worked as a labourer to make ends meet, and his mother sewed dresses, which she sold at local markets. Not that they needed the money – they were rich beyond imagination. Peter grew up surrounded by coins, jewellery and wads of banknotes. For as long as he could remember, this had always been there, tucked beneath the caravan's fold-away beds, at the bottom of cupboards, and in the cavity behind the broken stove. More money than could simply be explained away. More than a decent, modest couple had any business possessing.

Peter never asked where it came from, although his imagination toiled away looking for answers. Perhaps they had looted it from a vault split open by bombs or picked the spoils from the wreckage of people's lives. Neither did he question why they rarely spent any of it. He only ever asked one thing:

'Why can't we settle down?'

Peter asked this in sun-stricken meadows, in cool river valleys, and at night, beneath stars that were his only friends as his family moved from place to place. His father, a kindly white-haired man at fifty (the image of Peter as I knew him), smiled at him or handed him a marshmallow speared on a stick to roast over the embers of the cooking fire.

'We will,' he assured him always. 'Just as soon as we find the right place.'

They played out this scene again and again as the years passed. Peter always accepted his father's promise. When the fire's heat failed and the unshrouded sky sapped away all warmth, he went inside the caravan and fell asleep on his shelf. He often dreamed of luxurious beds with feather pillows and mattresses you could sink into. His parents had imposed this existence on him. He would accept it only so long as he had no other choice.

Each new place was supposed to be their last, but problems inevitably blighted them. In Aberdeen, they settled in open fields beneath grey winter skies but were ousted by the land's owners. In Cornwall, they found shelter in the shade of a sycamore, only to be overrun by sheep upon summer's commencement. Peter came to blame his parents for every little setback. It was their fault they kept uprooting. They didn't want to settle. They were happy living this half-life, alone in the wilderness with no friends or neighbours.

Peter's school changed with every season, as did the uniform. His mother modified his clothes with the skill of a master. Rarely did she give in and buy him anything new. She let down hems as he grew, and sewed up rips without leaving a mark. She conjured school badges from lengths of thread she kept in her craft box. It was a dainty thing made of polished wood and ivory. Peter remembered it vividly. There was a mirror inside the lid and a clockwork ballerina that twirled when the key was turned. The melody it played as the wooden girl danced sapped the life from him, conjuring images of stately homes inhabited only by fading tapestries and Georgian dolls, all sad and still, mourning the passing of the children that had once brought them to life. Peter's mother left the box open as she worked and hummed the tune to herself long after its spring wound down. Years later, he would remember her whenever those notes tumbled to the forefront of his mind. That association with lifeless buildings was replaced by a silent movie of his mother labouring in the sun, needle flashing, polished with use.

Peter's mother had work enough, keeping up with the demands of her son's growing body, not to mention the repair jobs necessitated by grass stains and rips. Every time Peter acquainted himself with a new school, he had the pleasure of being chased by a new set of bullies. Some pelted him with stones; others pursued him through woods until he tripped or twisted his ankle. He fought them with his fists sometimes, at others with barbed comments. In Wales, he found himself in a class of children who had lived there since birth and whose parents and parents had inhabited that same village before them. They took just one look at him, a wiry, pastel-skinned child, and labelled him 'impostor'. The little school adopted a hostile stance to this threat to their way of life, or at least to their gene pool. Similarly, Peter was quick to spot that everyone in town shared the same hair colour. He choked down his tears with mutters of 'inbreds'.

Peter eventually lost interest in making friends, realising he preferred his own company. He enjoyed reading about rocket engines and space shuttles. With only a radio for company – and its use was restricted to breakfast time – he had little else to capture his imagination.

Peter was sixteen when his parents found the place of their dreams. By then, he had heard it all before, so he set about scraping through the days without thinking too much about it. Why should Suffolk be different to anywhere else? They settled in Dunwich Heath, on the cliff tops, next to the sea. The sound of the surf permeated Peter's thoughts just as salt saturated his clothes. From the caravan window, he could see nothing but the sea and feel nothing but awe. A city stood once where the waves now ruled, a great port with countless churches whose bells had been silenced, except on misty mornings. The water had wiped streets, buildings and people away, leaving no trace of civilisation. Flat sea as far as the eye could see; it was like there never was such a city. A blank slate. Perfect forgiveness.

A few metres from the caravan, the ground dropped away, crashing to the rocky shore below. The cliffs were soft and prone to landslides, and the wind was relentless. This didn't deter Peter's parents. Their hearts were set. They felt an affinity with that cursed, forbidden earth.

People came around every day for the first few weeks.

They all wore thick jackets and worried expressions. Peter avoided them, choosing instead to wander along the base of the cliffs, exploring the shingle bed. Once, he chanced upon the remains of a seal washed up on the shore, black and rotting, eye sockets plucked of their jewels. He grabbed some driftwood and prodded its brittle skin until it split open and spilt out the poor creature's putrid insides. He stepped back, gagging but fascinated by these remnants of life.

High above him, teetering on the cliff's edge, stood fence posts and brickwork from buildings half-eaten, a landslide or two from oblivion. Tree roots jutted like the ribs of a felled beast whose flesh had been picked away by carrion.

Further up, towards the village, Peter happened across a churchyard – sanctified earth emptying into the sea. The church itself had been devoured in the early years of the century; one final tombstone remained. Such destruction astounded him. Sometimes, on those rare occasions when the wind was still and the tide was out, it was easier for him to believe that man, not nature, was to blame for the carnage.

Peter's father must have shared that same illusion. He wanted to build a house on the strip of land atop the cliffs. It was to be the most magnificent construction, with thick, red-bricked walls that would fortify the rock that was eroding around it. It would become a buttress against the elements. And yet, this place was fated to have the consistency of a dream. Their home remained a mirage, its roaring fires, thick blankets and feather pillows a reality only in their minds.

It was gusty as Peter walked home from school that night. He was accustomed to this, but it had never, in his experience, been quite that bad. His teacher had kept referring to the Great East Storm a decade earlier, which had flooded the school and plucked oak trees from the ground. Autumn leaves whipped across the street, spearing themselves on skeletal hedges. Nobody cycled anywhere that day. Pedestrians fought their way along the pavement. Old men pressed down on their caps, women's skirts whipped and bellowed, and mothers gripped toddlers' arms tightly.

Peter relegated all this to the periphery of his consciousness. Tonight was the night. He had planned this for months, from its initial formulation as a silly idea to something he had convinced himself made sense.

He was going to run away.

Peter's parents were out walking. They did this regularly before dusk. They spent long summer evenings at the foot of the cliffs, erecting a windbreaker and settling into their books, epic nineteenth-century affairs, novels that you did not so much read as accompany. They were probably down on the gravel beach somewhere. The waves thundered – nature was flexing its muscles – yet they did not retreat, convinced as they were that only man could harm them.

This was his opportunity. The weather hadn't changed their plans, so why should it change his?

Peter went inside the caravan and emptied his school satchel onto the floor. He then filled it up again with clothes and tins of food from the cupboards. He would need money, of course, but that would not be a problem. His little hands rooted around the cavities, fumbling for every last note and coin. He was fairly sure he wouldn't miss anything. After all, he had spent his whole life in that confined space. He knew where the cash was; he knew every nook and cranny.

This was the first act in a sequence of events which I have never been able to fathom entirely. It is easy enough for me to gloss over this, though, because everything is over-shadowed by the final image in this tale. As far as I can tell, Peter's parents must have returned and spotted him with the money. They must have argued. Peter must have told them he didn't need them anymore, before turning his back on them and bursting out of the caravan with a heavy satchel of loot slung over his shoulder.

Rain pelted him. It came in horizontally from the sea. Peter shielded his eyes. For a moment, he was blind. He stumbled towards the village, buffeted by the wind. The next thing he heard was a terrible sucking noise from far below. The wind had created a vortex at the foot of the cliffs, a chance happening, a freak of nature, an act of God. The storm seemed at once to have gained great purpose, channelling its energies into one monstrous act. It knocked him down easily, screaming in his ears. He landed in the mud, where he was safe with his stolen treasure.

When setting up the caravan, his parents had weighed it down with bricks. This had seen it through countless windy days. This storm was something else. The wind gnashed its teeth and rocked its new toy back and forth until, finally, the caravan turned on its side. The sucking noise intensified. Peter's eardrums squealed.

He willed his parents to climb out, to kick through a window and crawl to safety. They never did. He shouted to them but couldn't hear his voice over the racket. He tried to move, but a gust pinned him down.

And that final image? The caravan slid through the mud towards the cliff's edge. There was nothing in its way. The thin grass scraped away in clumps as it carved a deep gouge into the earth. As it gained momentum, plastic splintered, and walls crumpled. Finally, the ground deserted it.

It disappeared into the night.

# Chapter 11

## *Contact*

My father would have preferred to have a sporty son. He was obsessed with football and bought goalposts for me as a present so we could have a knockabout in the garden. I never encouraged him in this endeavour. I probably wouldn't even if I hadn't had a heart condition. I associated team sports too much with clumsy male bonding – you know, fathers dragging their sons out to matches, regardless of rain, sleet or snow. I saw something inherently primitive, too, in aligning yourself to a clan with a club scarf and football strip and deriving meaning from a sport so rooted in yob culture.

This contact meeting with my father would probably have seemed less intimidating if we'd had something like that in common, a shared language, something to bridge the divide. What exactly were we supposed to do together, anyway – sit there and stare at each other, talk about the weather and tell anecdotes about amusing incidents from my childhood? That wasn't exactly my idea of quality time. Worse still was the prospect of having to talk to my father about domestic arrangements. I really wanted to keep that off the table! What if he started talking to me about what had happened? What might he say, what excuses might he try? *'When she looked at me sometimes, I could see the kind of man I'd become. I could see that I'd failed her. I couldn't stand it, so I just lashed out.'* Just the thought of it was pathetic.

My father was, to me, always a man's man. Soul-searching wasn't his style. The only thing he appreciated was force. I was nothing like him. Except once, just a few days before that contact meeting, when I let myself go.

Brian and I were getting lunch out of our lockers ahead of chess club. We had just completed a gruelling Home Economics lesson, baking cakes. Mine had refused point-blank to rise, but Brian had produced this magnificent triple-chocolate creation coated with *Maltesers*, marshmallows and almonds. He had named it 'Diabetics Nightmare', much to the dismay of our insulin-dependent classmate, Jade Broadsmith.

Brian was telling me something, but I wasn't paying much attention. He had been going on about his cake for the past ten minutes, gloating about how much better than mine it was, yet refusing to cut me a slice. Cake first, talk later; that was my position. Maybe I should have tried harder to listen, considering the effort I had put into getting back in his good books. Then again, I hadn't been listening to anyone that week. I just couldn't. My mind kept wandering, dragging me to the doors of the Hog's Head, my father's local. He was inside, but I wasn't sure whether or not I wanted to see him, so I waited there as summer waned, autumn shrivelled, and winter's snow covered over everything. I was trapped in that melancholy world.

Brian bashed into me, knocking me into my locker. My forehead crashed into it so hard that the door dented. Something rattled around my skull. I turned and scowled at him. I was just about to bite his head off when I realised he was just as disoriented as me.

As my senses came back online, I could hear laughter. Five of them – two boys and three girls – were cackling like jackals. They were already at the other end of the corridor. They must have shoved Brian into me, setting off a domino effect that climaxed with me becoming intimately acquainted with the surface of my locker door. I recognised the gang from the gathering at Anna Duverman's house. They were the trendy ones, the life and the soul of the party. In their midst was everyone's favourite head boy, Sean Frankley, who held on his arm his girlfriend of the week.

Brian wasn't bullied by a specific group –it was more a societal movement than a local feud – but it was surprising to see such an auspicious bunch involved. I had rarely seen them take an interest in anything or anyone outside of their own clique. Getting them to acknowledge your existence was something, never mind getting them to persecute you actively. I don't know what about Brian held him up for this special attention, but it could almost have been something to brag about.

I didn't ponder this then: I was too busy pursuing them. I pushed through the crowd of kids at their lockers. I don't know what was going through my head. Had I even considered that this might not be the best of ideas?

When I caught up with my targets, they were about to head outside. I grabbed Sean by the shoulder. That got his attention.

'Why did you do that?' I demanded.

They were stunned, all five of them. His girlfriend,

Natalie, stopped chewing her gum. A rare occurrence, indeed.

I held my ground, glaring at Sean. It felt exhilarating, not scary at all.

Then I realised that I was looking up at quite a considerable angle. Sean was tall and pretty beefy, to boot. He worked out. I hadn't noticed this before. Standing so close to him, nose to nose (or nose to square chin, to be accurate), it was hard to avoid. His shoulders were broad. Muscles, not flab, bulked out his shirt. I began to lose my nerve.

Sean smirked. 'For a minute there, I thought you were going to make something of it, Farlowe.'

I was a little flattered that Sean knew my name. It turned out that he knew a lot more about me than that:

'I thought you had some of your father's blood in you.'

'Your Dad's a nutter,' added the other male in the group, for whom inference was not a concept.

This guy was considerably bigger, even than Sean. He had a crew cut and a permanently bewildered expression. I think he was called Warren or something. A henchman's name, if ever there was one.

Then Sean came back with, 'Almost banged up in Littlehay a few years back, wasn't he?'

I just stood there. This was the first I'd heard of my father having any kind of reputation, but then again, I had never given anyone a reason to employ it against me before. I couldn't remember my father ever being close to a prison sentence, but maybe my parents had shielded me from that. Lied to me.

'Doesn't look like it runs in the family,' said Warren. 'Look at him.'

Sean snorted. 'I bet his Daddy lays him across his knee

and spanks him every night to show him what a little bitch he is.'

And I was gone. I don't know what happened, but I completely lost it. I launched at Sean. Suddenly, I hated him more than anyone else in the world.

Sean might have been bigger than me, but I had the element of surprise. I barged shoulder-first into his stomach. Caught off guard, he collided with the wall. He gasped for breath, mouthing like a goldfish. That had shut him up.

I stepped back, alive with victory.

Then I felt an arm around my neck. It tightened, crushing my windpipe. Warren had me in a headlock. I struggled to get away, but he was way too strong – all I succeeded in doing was hurting myself.

Warren manoeuvred so that my head was tucked beneath his armpit. I was bent right over, totally in his power. It was demeaning. And I needed air. I really needed air!

My heartbeat was a platoon of soldiers marching in my ears. As the seconds passed, my brain seemed to swell, pressing against the inside of my skull. Everything grew distant. I could tell we had an audience, and I could hear them chanting, 'Fight, fight, fight!' but that was it.

Warren juggled me from one arm to the other, freeing up a hand to slap me on the bum. The mob cheered.

By this point, Sean had recovered from my attack. I could just about see him adjusting his school tie. He was grinning again.

He nodded to Warren, and finally, I was freed. I staggered around, scanning the grim, fascinated faces of the crowd, silently pleading for someone to help. Where was Brian when I needed him?

Sean ambled up and kicked me behind the knees. I

crumpled to the floor. Then he started putting his boot in. Again and again, his shoes sunk into my side. From the feel of them, they were steel-capped. I was in such pain that I didn't make a sound. I just cowered and endured it.

'You... do not... do that ... to me!' Sean emphasised each word with a kick. 'Understand?'

I thought that would be the last of it, but then Warren pulled me to my feet. I was so sore that part of me felt like slumping, but I was still wild with fury, even if my body wasn't built for it.

Warren backed off. I looked Sean square in the face.

'Come on,' he said, amused by my defiance. 'Give me your best shot.'

At this point, Brian appeared from a classroom. Mr Adams, my history teacher, wasn't far behind. He was shouting something.

But by then, it was too late. All the anger, all the frustration, and all the humiliation boiled up inside me and I was oblivious to everything else.

My memories from that point on are a series of images:

The flash of disbelief in Sean's eyes.

The crunch of my fist against his nose.

The explosion of pain as bone hit bone.

Then, the rest of it is a blur – all shouting, blood and guilt. The next thing I knew, Sean was being carted off to the sick room, and I was being escorted to see the headmaster.

* * *

I waited outside the headmaster's office for at least fifteen minutes, with nothing else to do but consider my fate.

People kept slipping in and out of the office, casting

cursory glances in my direction as they passed. This made me feel pretty small, the only student consigned to the silent, timeless corridors of the school admin section.

I studied my knuckles. They were red and raw, and beginning to swell. I couldn't stretch my fingers out properly. I looked up every time I heard footsteps, hoping that someone would be able to tell me about Sean. Was he okay? What had I done?

It all felt surreal, tucked away in isolation after what had happened. I could still hear the fight – the chanting, the rush of blood – raging in my ears. My heart was still beating hard (dangerously hard, considering my condition), and my shirt was soaked through. This wasn't me. What I'd done wasn't me. It felt easier to question the memory than to accept it. But there was no escaping reality. I was becoming my father. Not in some abstract way, but in flesh, in thought and in deed; in this body that I could no longer control.

I waited there in limbo.

The headmaster seemed irritable when he eventually called me in. He didn't say my name. He just held the door open and gestured for me to enter.

His name was Mr Spencer. In many ways, he reminded me of Tony Blair, in that he had been youthful and dynamic when first taking over the post, but the responsibility had made him haggard, and grey hairs had sprung amongst his black. His skin was tired and pockmarked, as though it had been struck by thousands of tiny meteors. It was strange to see him at such close quarters. Normally, he was a distant figure in assembly, prattling on about study skills, commitment, hope and the future.

I noticed that his tie was loose.

Stepping into his office was like taking a trip back to the height of the British Empire. A giant Union Jack covered an entire wall. It looked thick and expensive, like it had been handed to him folded by the Queen. A world map was framed behind his desk. It was so yellowed that I could imagine it being used to chart troop movements during the Second World War. Britain was right in the centre. The chairs were coated with buffed leather, stretched tight over high backs. A faint smell of tobacco hung in the air, the kind you get when you open an old book that your grandparents used to own.

Mr Spencer closed the door behind me and indicated that I should sit. I obeyed wordlessly, totally disarmed by my surroundings. He then proceeded to reel off some great long speech about violence, crime and responsibility. He used the word 'unacceptable' several times while pacing around his office. It was all very rehearsed, as though he had gone through this a thousand times before. I could tell that he meant what he was saying – he was an able public speaker who could command attention – but he wasn't angry. There was no bite to his words. I didn't fear him, as I did my father.

This seemed like an inconvenience to him, like he had a thousand better things to do.

'Behaviour like that,' he said, 'betrays a fundamental lack of respect for your peers. You have let down the school and the teachers, who work so hard to make it a safe place. You have let down your peers, your parents, and most of all, you have let down yourself.'

I tried to fight it as my face turned red, but I couldn't stop the tears. Water leaked down the sides of my nose. I brushed it away, but that only increased the flow.

Mr Spencer had noticed, but this didn't stop him from continuing. He was in full swing, I suppose, going through the motions. He had to stop in the end, though: I was sobbing so loudly that it became apparent I couldn't hear a word he was saying.

He sat on the other side of his desk and waited a few minutes for me to calm down. He pushed a box of tissues towards me.

'What you did was serious, Nick.'

Hearing him say my name made a big difference. He was now talking to me, not some generic troublemaker.

'I understand that you were provoked,' he continued, 'and that it's easy to lose your head in the midst of things. But you've got to learn when to stop. A teacher was there. That should have been it. Time to stop.'

He looked at me as I dried my eyes. I realised he was expecting a response, so I nodded in agreement.

'Good,' he said. 'I'm going to be lenient on this occasion. Understand that this privilege will not be afforded again. Two week's after-school detention with your tutor.'

I nodded again.

Mr Spencer strode to his door and opened it for me.

'Don't take your eye off the ball,' he said as I left.

That was the one time I got in trouble with the 'powers that be'. It was probably also the only time I came close to being my true self, to let myself go, free of inhibitions. It wouldn't happen again. I had scared myself.

For the next few days, I was constantly aware of a rage within me, bubbling beneath the surface, a primal instinct that threatened to explode again at any moment. I kept thinking back to times when I had lost my temper, tantrums I'd thrown as a toddler – all those embarrassing toys-out-of-pram incidents – and more recently, when I had snapped all the pencils in my room. I tried to justify these outbursts to myself, but all I succeeded in doing was painting myself a monster. There seemed very little difference between them and those incidents when my father had lost it and lashed out at Mum. It was just a matter of scale.

He was the key, wasn't he? He had become a spectre, infecting every part of my personality. I was unaware of the crimes that had gained him infamy, but they had left their mark on me, somehow.

It wasn't just his apparent right to see me that bothered me, but the inescapability of biology. I was half my mother and half my father; none of me was my own. Nobody's allowed our own personality: we're just bits and pieces of our relatives' characters amalgamated into one. It's as arbitrary as the fusion of our parents' DNA strands.

Why couldn't I just be me?

The contact meeting that Saturday was hanging over me big time. That whole week felt like a build-up to it. And Mum didn't help. I went down one morning and found the *'Which Guide to Divorce'* left out on the breakfast table. It felt like she was choosing a new life – my new life – like a holiday home.

I got up at about half seven on Saturday morning on the day I was set to meet my father and got my bike out of the garage. Dawn was breaking. The air was crisp, unaccustomed to being breathed. Every surface had a twinkle to it: roads, walls and fence posts. When I arrived at the river, I noticed that the discarded Coke cans and crisp packets on the path's edge were furry with frost. A mist hovered about two feet above the grass of the Backs, barely touched by the sun, which was impossible to place in the white sky.

I followed the river downstream as best I could. Our paths diverged in the town centre, but I caught up with it by the boathouses, where I used to meet Peter. I carried on along the towpath. I was searching for a place he had described to me.

This was the first time I had ridden my new bike. The seat was set too low, making cycling tough, but by the time I realised this, I was too far from home to go back and adjust it. I had wrapped up warm, and my heart was pounding from the exercise, but my fingers still turned numb, and my face stung from the cold's bite.

I wasn't in a hurry, so I slowed down to keep pace with one of the boats of university students heading out to practice. All eight rowers moved as one, straining to propel the boat through the heavy water. They tried to look cool and relaxed, but their cheeks were red, and their foreheads glistened. Their cox shouted encouragement through a loudspeaker: '*Wind up, wind up!*' and '*Stride, stride!*'

I lost track of the boat as the cycle path crossed the river and deposited me in a housing estate. I had entered the village-cum-suburb of Chesterton. Its inhabitants were beginning to rise. I could see the glow of morning television through net curtains. The streetlights had dimmed, first to red, then to nothing.

After a few minutes, I re-joined the river on a bumpy path. Every stone I rode over jolted me, despite my bike's suspension. The frost had solidified footprints in the mud. The vibration started to jar my back, so I changed down a few gears and slowed to a walking pace. So much for the fabled shock absorbers!

I kept going beneath the railway and the concrete A14 bridge, stopping finally where the river turned towards Bait Bite Lock. I had been cycling for the best part of an hour by then. The sky had gained definition, blue and white wavering in the water. Everywhere I looked, the land was flat. The field across the river stretched as far as I could see, a vast wasteland thinly carpeted with grass needles. Power lines zigzagged across it, their destination unclear in places; in others, they headed, confident and determined, towards a lone cottage or a collection of buildings or back towards Cambridge.

The wind was dominant here. It whipped up, unhindered, whistling in my ears.

What made me stop there? On first impressions, it was no different from the stretches of riverbank I had already passed through. But Peter had described this place to me in detail, particularly the tree I stood by now, which had split in two. It was the most incredible sight. Its thick limbs were torn apart by their own weight, exposing its golden flesh slowly succumbing to fungus. Similar trees nearby had avoided this fate by entwining their boughs, supporting each other. This one had stretched its arms out wide, grasping for the sky with such enthusiasm that its very structure had failed.

I had met with Peter the night before, having run there straight from detention, late but unwilling to confess why. I had just panted and slumped onto the bench. Peter had carried on as usual, taking me straight into the Lord's Prayer. I had to interrupt him. I just couldn't sit still, couldn't regulate my breaths, couldn't even do that.

'I'm sorry,' I said, fidgeting. 'Give me a second.'

Peter gaped at me as though I had murdered someone.

'You don't have the discipline to say the Lord's Prayer with me?' he said.

'I'm sorry,' I repeated, searching for excuses. 'It's just that I've been at school all day. It takes me a moment to get into the right frame of mind.'

Peter kept me firmly in his gaze whilst weighing up

what I'd just said. It may have been an excuse, but it wasn't a lie. There were so many different things going on in my life at that time that I had taken to compartmentalising them. It usually took me a while to get back into the 'Peter mindset', which was far removed from that of friends and family.

'I see,' Peter said, and I realised he would let me off the hook. 'I, too, used to find it difficult to see God sometimes. I was reading so much, just as you are now, learning all the time, and it was difficult to keep my heart on the only thing that truly mattered, which was my relationship with Christ.'

Peter proceeded to tell me to follow the river out of the city on the old towpath. Out in the open, where the hustle-bustle that fills our lives can be mistaken for a breeze, this was where he went to be with God.

This was the place.

I propped my bike against the tree, opened my back-pack and pulled out a packet of *Wotsits*. I stood there wolfing them down, awaiting epiphany. It's difficult to say whether it arrived in the end or not. Certainly, the solitude did do something to alter my state of consciousness. As minutes passed, the concerns that had claimed my attention dropped away. My life, as I knew it, grew distant, as though I was peering at it through a misty window. In that place, I escaped the whirlwind of activity that filled my days.

I'm well aware that I haven't done justice to the experience, but I can't go into much more detail than that. That sounds like a cop-out, but language only stretches so far. Forget about words. Forget about light bulbs, central heating, and the whine of muted televisions, the everyday of civilisation. If I could write twenty paragraphs of words that catch in the throat and can never be uttered, I would be getting close to what I felt there. That silence. And that sky.

Confronted by the enormity of wilderness, I became more than the sum of my experiences. I stopped living, stopped thinking, and just was.

I go to that place still, whenever I'm back in Cambridge visiting my mother. The time between visits seems to lack consequence when I'm there. It crumples up. Faces and places merge into an over-exposed snapshot of the days since my last visit. This is how I mark the passage of my life.

Sending me there and telling me about that place was probably the greatest thing Peter ever did for me.

After an indeterminable length of time, a man and a woman came along. They were holding hands and seemed so into each other that they might not have noticed me. All the same, I grew self-conscious. I grabbed my bike and cycled home.

It was well after midday by the time I got back. I had been supposed to meet my father at half past ten.

## Chapter 12

---

### *Winter's Depth*

Christmas crept up on me that year. Partly, this was because no one gave me an advent calendar. I'd had one every year until then, with chocolate-flavoured treats behind each window, encouraging me to count the days and teasing me with tasters of the overindulgence that would follow. Anticipation usually made December hellish. My parents used to wrap my presents early, too. They laid them out under the tree in a prime position for prodding. It was unbearable.

Not so that year. Mum didn't even mention Christmas. I began to wonder if we were going to celebrate it at all. Christmas is a family time, isn't it? I wasn't part of a proper family anymore. We were just individuals trying our best to extricate ourselves from legal and emotional bonds, straying ever closer to having nothing at all to do with each other.

Everything was still up in the air on that front. Mum didn't bother to arrange any further contact meetings with my father. This suited me fine. From then on, the only contact I would have with him were brief exchanges on the telephone, when he had to speak with her about an administrative matter. 'Is your Mum there?' he'd say. 'I'll get her,' my reply.

I had assumed Mum would be pleased that I didn't want to see my father, but when it came to it, she painted my actions in a light I had never even considered. She told me I had disappointed her and that she'd hoped we were close enough to talk about things without me feeling I needed to run off like that. She cornered me with this as soon as I got back. Any trace of liberation I felt after my trip down the river quickly dissipated.

A social worker paid a visit a week or so after the aborted meeting. She asked me a few questions but seemed satisfied when I told her I just wanted to get on with my life.

'He needs to work through a few things,' I overheard her telling Mum afterwards. 'He needs space, but also assurance that you're there for him if he needs you.'

'I just want to do the right thing,' Mum said.

On the school front, let's start with a positive: I hadn't actually broken Sean's nose. I had expected to see him bandaged up like a plastic surgery victim, but nothing so dramatic. The school nurse had taken him to hospital purely to cover her own back. When I next saw him (a glimpse down the corridor as I moved swiftly between class-rooms, head lowered), his nose was all bruised. It was so swollen that it looked like its ambition was to conquer his entire face. I felt terrible about it. Still, it could have been a lot worse. If it had been broken... well, to me (and probably also to the other parties involved), that would have moved my crime up to a different level, from playground incident to full-blown assault.

I had been thinking a lot about the fight, considering that, in a way, it had been kind of a letdown. Having sat through plenty of action movies, I had a fair idea of what a fight should look like: heroes and villains battling in stunningly choreographed scenes whilst exchanging pithy one-liners. Fighting is an art; it is refined and acceptable in its context. Ours was more of a scrap: clumsy, messy and without artistic merit. Not that it left any less of an impression on me for that. The violence was real, not abstract. Outside Hollywood, a blow meant soreness for days to come. And it wasn't acceptable, not in any way at all.

Nobody at school wanted anything to do with me. People with whom I had occasionally swapped an idle comment or two now blanked me completely. Entire crowds parted for me as I walked down corridors. This had the benefit of halving my journey time from one lesson to the next, but it was an eerie feeling, like in those old Westerns when a stranger walks down Main Street of a dusty town, to the sound of shutters being closed and nervous-looking mothers ushering their kids inside. For the first time in my life, I sensed eyes on me. I was a celebrity. But it wasn't admiration I felt in those stares.

Looking back, I was imagining a lot of stuff. What I'd done had impacted as much on my self-perception as that of others. I felt dangerous. I carried myself differently, I'm sure of it.

As for Sean, nobody took him seriously as head boy after that. He painted himself as the innocent victim in this, but most people knew what had really happened, and he had lost credibility. No one could reconcile Sean's role in the fight with the nice-guy image he had taken care to construct for himself. People started looking beyond appearances and didn't like what they saw. This gave me some small satisfaction.

Maybe everything would return to normal after the Christmas break, when my outburst would no longer be news, and everyone would have different tales to tell. But I still had to get through a couple more weeks of school.

Another positive: none of the other kids ever bothered Brian again. Not that he ever thanked me for it.

Okay, so there was quite a bit of good news. Sam, Michael and Brian stuck by me, too. Whether this was the result of conscious solidarity, habit, or a concerted effort to fly in the face of mass opinion, I couldn't say. But I appreciated it. I never thought I would say it, but being with my friends really helped. Michael, in particular, was good to me. He kept lending me CDs. I didn't ask him for them; he just took it upon himself to take me to one side now and then and thrust one into my hands.

'Listen to this,' he would say. 'It makes sense of everything.' Or: 'Track 4 must be the greatest song ever recorded. Aside from *Desolation Row*, that is.'

Michael's songs were mainly singer-songwriter stuff, and they didn't have the impact they might have. Sure, they were heartfelt and earnest, but all their sentiment seemed second-hand, like messages in greeting cards. I concluded that they had been spoilt by the very fact that he had loaned them to me. These were the kind of songs that you need to discover for yourself. Songs that mean something to me these days are stray thoughts pinned down with melody, ideas from the edge of sleep, given substance by music. They are snippets of life, linked inextricably with past events that will stay with me forever – the things that were on my mind when I first played them, the people I was with, the good or bad times we shared. Songs, to me, are lovers that time can't change, compensation for girlfriends I've never had. The problem with these songs was that Michael was imprinted himself on them. How could I develop a relationship with them when I knew he cherished them first?

This didn't prevent us from entering into a musical debate. Michael kept coming up with these weird projects to show off his knowledge. I didn't have a clue what he was talking about half the time, but I played along, grateful that we had something more in common than a love of computer games and science fiction. I remember once, he was trying to compile a list of albums that summed up the concept of Britishness. This threw up several points of contention, chief among them being the inclusion of both *Chumbawumba* and *Stone Roses*.

'I think they sum up your quintessential football hooligan,' explained Michael. 'Important part of British culture, that. Especially for people organising sporting events.'

'Okay, I accept that,' I said, 'but you can't have both. Remember the rule – one band per category.'

Michael sighed. 'Are you still sore about me making you choose between *Pulp* and *Divine Comedy*? Get over it, will you?'

'I don't care about that,' I said. 'Look at this list – you've got *Divine Comedy* as "English Country Fop", *The Rolling Stones* representing "British Sexual Prowess", *Radiohead* as "Tortured Social Conscience", *S Club 7* for "Everything bad about British pop music today". One for everything. You can't have two for "Hooliganism."'

'Just you watch me.'

We jostled over this for ages before reaching a compromise. Michael dumped *Chumbawumba* on the grounds that they were crap, and invented another section entitled 'British Troublemaker', within which he placed *Oasis*. And, just to please me (although I swear, I didn't care), he reintroduced Pulp as 'Voice of the Unshaven Classes'. Michael occasionally surrendered ground like that to keep me interested and maintain the illusion that I had something to contribute. And – make no mistake about it – it *was* an illusion. Michael lived and breathed music; I had other things going on.

After-school detentions were taking up a lot of my time. In all my years of going to school (which would have been about eleven by then), I had never been in detention. It wasn't that I was a model student or anything. I was just good at blending into the background. I had developed the ability to say 'Sir' in a slurred, sardonic tone that wasn't respectful, but that was as far as my rebellious instinct went. I viewed those hours of forfeited time as a rite of passage. I found it strangely comforting sitting there serving my time with other people my age. I had expected a traumatic affair, with my tutor, Mr Kendall, shouting at us for twenty minutes flat. In the event, all he did was sit preparing the next day's lessons while we got on with our homework in silence.

My fellow inmates came and went as I served my time. For the first few days, I was accompanied by Marcus Campbell, who had a history of setting off the fire alarm during double science. Now, this guy really didn't like physics. He didn't like anything much. Well, nothing school-related. He never did any work in detention. He just sat there scowling at me and picking his nose (anatomically, two very difficult actions to combine, believe me), re-housing the contents of his nostrils on the underside of the table.

Next came Derek Norman. I hadn't talked to him before, although we were in a lot of the same classes. I hadn't been missing much. Derek had no sense of humour whatsoever. I'm not saying I'm the funniest person in the world, but come on, he could have at least smiled at me, just to be polite! I never discovered why he was in detention.

Whenever I asked, he smiled cryptically and tapped the side of his nose.

Then there was Jo. She joined me in the second week, having secured a place on our little chain gang by calling Mr Kendall a 'fascist arsehole'. Not the subtlest of insults, she admitted.

'He leaned over me,' she informed me in a hurriedly written note, slid across the table, 'and told me I'm a no-hoper at maths. Apparently, I don't apply myself. I had a splitting headache, so I told him where to stick it.'

I sniggered. Mr Kendall looked up. Jo and I pretended to be hard at work. A little while later, when his attention was elsewhere, I wrote back:

'Everyone has a right to be crap at maths. But maybe you could have reacted better.'

'Do you think I should have smacked him on the nose instead?'

I had no reply to that.

So Jo. Jo, Jo, Jo. It must have been around then that I started to realise that I enjoyed her company. There was something special about her, something I had only just noticed. Sure, Brian used to tease us about sexual tension, but he had just been joking, hadn't he? I had never seriously thought for one second that she or I might want to... you know, do anything. But things were different now. I wasn't sure why, but sitting next to her in detention was exciting and kind of pleasant. I don't think I had ever felt that before. I told myself I was just glad for the company but was fully aware that it was more than that.

Things between us progressed slowly. I walked her home after school, even though she lived miles away from me, in the other direction. Neither of us commented on this. I think we were both reticent to say anything explicitly. We skirted around the issue until Jo confronted me on one particularly icy night:

'Haven't you got anywhere better to be?'

We were at her garden gate. I checked my watch. It wasn't even six yet. Mum wouldn't be home for a couple of hours.

'Um, no,' I said. All right, Peter had given me plenty to read, and my coursework wasn't going to write itself, but neither seemed more pressing than walking Jo back home.

Jo smiled and brushed back a strand of her frizzy hair, brittle from the black dye she had used to stain it. 'Well, I would invite you in, but – you know – the family. I try to keep everyone away from them as much as possible.'

'I can understand that,' I said. 'You should meet mine.'

I learned a lot about Jo that week. I discovered, for example, that Anna – the raving socialite whose party I had crashed only to sit dejectedly in the kitchen – was only Jo's half-sister. Jo was the illegitimate daughter of some German inventor whom her mother refused to name. This explained a lot. It had been difficult to believe that Jo and Anna shared the same blood.

Jo's ignorance about her parentage didn't seem to bother her. She thrived on it. Having done her research, she claimed descent from every famous German inventor, from Karlheinz Brandenburg and Bernhard Grill (the MP3) to Felix Wankel (the Rotary Cylinder Engine). Limiting herself to only one father – someone who had invented something obscure, like an automatic toenail clipper or a racket-string tightener – would have ruined this.

I discovered also that Jo was a keen environmentalist. She spent her weekends volunteering, maintaining foot-paths and netting litter from the river. That was nice. She loved animals, too, except for the squirrel. Bloody squirrels', she said whenever anything went wrong. She blamed them for everything: they laddered her tights, hid her homework and messed with her hair as she slept. A half-remembered childhood trauma was clearly surfacing. I decided not to explore it too deeply.

It is amazing all the little facts about people that you don't pick up unless you make a specific effort to listen. With Jo, I made that effort, and I got something back. I could feel us developing some connection. Both of us were aware that something could happen, but I hadn't a clue how to trigger it. Sometimes, we brushed against each other by accident, or our hands touched on the railings as we pushed our way up a packed school staircase. That felt weird enough. The idea of touching her purposefully – of kissing her even – was unthinkable.

It seemed obvious to me that the onus was on me to do something. To this end, I tripled the amount of TV I watched, hoping to catch a romantic moment and get an idea of how it was done. I sat through several episodes of *Neighbours*, looking for clues, but something got lost in translation. I couldn't picture myself sidling across a beach to this nubile young woman and interrupting her while she was putting on her sun-tan lotion by asking, 'Can I help you with that, mate?' (or Sheila, whatever).

Okay, so maybe my recollections of *Neighbours* are a bit vague.

At the end of a week of TV viewing, I concluded that I didn't have a hope of ensnaring Jo unless we were being pursued by the Russian mafia, subverting the tyrannical rule of the Sheriff of Nottingham, or standing with arms outstretched on the prow of the Titanic. I couldn't imagine any of these scenarios coming to pass in the near future.

And so, on the last day of term, Jo and I bid farewell to

each other as usual: a brief nod, nothing more. Our little romance was definitely a case of 'to be continued'.

What with everything else that was going on, I only saw Peter twice in those weeks. TV soaps replaced my Bible studies. I tried to force myself to keep reading about Christ, but something always got in the way. It all seemed too heavy.

I took Peter a scarf and some gloves the second time I went to see him: gifts to make up for my general crapness. Winter deepened with every night; we were fast approaching the solstice. Peter had taken to wearing a jacket donated to the night shelter, but it wasn't enough. Every day and every night, Peter was just one more patch of warmth to be subdued. Any little thing I could do to help counted for something.

I met Peter at our usual spot and handed the woollens over. He didn't smile or thank me. He just looked up and nodded, slipped the gloves on, and returned to writing in his book. I was late again.

I sat down next to him on the bench. The air was so cold that our breaths condensed as they passed our lips, masking our faces. I didn't want to hang around needlessly, but I knew that any effort to hurry Peter would be entirely counter-productive.

I tried to glance at his book. He snapped it shut.

'I have been worrying,' he said, stretching his legs. His toes cracked like fallen twigs.

'Look, I'm sorry I'm late,' I said. 'I got held up at school.'

'It worries me what has happened to us as a society,' Peter continued. 'Over the past century, we have strayed far from the Lord's path. So rarely do I see true devotion. There is just apathy and commercialism – just the grind of life. This is not God's way.'

Was he talking about me? I was the first to admit that I had started to lose my focus, but I couldn't exactly be blamed for a hundred years of societal change.

'I cannot believe that the Lord wants us to express our devotion to him through violence,' Peter said, 'but there must be a middle ground. This apathy is the greatest insult. Does anybody now care about anything? This thing called Christmas, this celebration of God becoming flesh, means nothing to them. The mention of Christ at this festival is incidental. This troubles me.'

I didn't want to argue with him. 'I suppose Christmas is about lots of different things these days.'

'Family and Christmases past,' Peter spat. 'Mulled wine and log fires. Tradition. What they celebrate is meaningless. Christ came to save our souls. Is that not enough?'

I wiped my nose. I probably agreed with Peter but couldn't get myself worked up about it. I was as big a culprit as anybody. Christmas had little to do for me with Christ, especially that year when it had more relevance as a mile-stone – the first Christmas without my father.

It occurred to me then, for the first time, that this thing with Peter might not work out. I was grateful to him for opening my eyes to what God might be like, but I wasn't sure how much further he could take me. Our lives were so different. If I were to find God, it would be another than Peter's.

I wasn't a good Christian. That's what it came down to. I wasn't bred for that stuff. This couldn't have been plainer than when I had punched Sean. Peter's way necessitated piety and self-control. I would never be like him – it wasn't in my genes. Christ wouldn't heed the likes of me; I had no place reserved in Heaven. Wouldn't it be better if I just accepted that and moved on?

'Look,' I said. 'I'm not sure I can do this anymore.'

Peter had taken in another breath to continue his rant, but he came to a spluttering stop. His eyes bulged. 'What do you mean?'

Should I say it, or shouldn't I? Before I knew it, my mouth was already moving. 'I'm not cut out for this. I'm not a Christian.'

Peter was silent for a while. When he spoke again, his voice was softer:

'None of us are good Christians, my son. We live in a sinful world. All we can do is live our lives the best we can and pray to God for the rest. If we are worthy, He will save us. We must battle this flesh.' He pinched the grey skin of one cheek. 'It anchors us to the material. It drags us towards lust and Satan's domain.'

'I've tried,' I said. 'Believe me, I've tried. I've read and read and read, and I know it must all fit together somehow. But it's all just information. It doesn't make me believe.'

Peter removed a glove and reached out with a stone-cold hand to touch my forehead, right where I had been christened as an infant. It took all my willpower to stop myself recoiling.

'Your sight is clouded by the Devil's tricks,' he said. 'Satan wants you to pick away at it with logic, to be guided by your brain rather than your soul. True understanding is beyond our capacity as human beings. Science is the Dark One's greatest weapon because it fosters the expectation of proof. You cannot *explain* God; you cannot *rationalise* Him; you must simply believe. That is the least the Lord asks of you. If you have faith, the Lord will find you, and all will fall into place.'

'But I can't make myself believe,' I objected. 'It just won't happen.'

Peter studied me for a while then, weighing me up, just as he had done all those weeks ago before giving me his Bible. What was there to look at? What was he looking for that he had not already seen?

'Listen to me,' he said at last.

And he told me his tale.

## Chapter 13

—————

### *The Lie*

Peter made his fortune in London, building an empire with the money he stole from his parents. At eighteen, he opened a corner shop; in his early twenties, he started a firm manufacturing aircraft parts. This went on to notch up contracts with several major airlines.

Peter threw himself into materialism, mind, body and spirit. One of the main attractions of this career path was that it was a direct challenge to the technology-shunning lifestyle of his parents, which had made his youth so miserable. They would have hated the way he was living his life. In his own small way, Peter was reaching for the stars, as had done his childhood idols from the Gemini and Apollo missions (their names had been banned in his household). Science was a dark pleasure.

He was powerful and could buy anything he wanted. He lived in a penthouse apartment overlooking the Thames. His office, where he spent most of his time, was huge, too. His name and title, 'Chief Executive', was emblazoned boldly on its glass door. Subtlety was not a word in his vocabulary. He had a secretary, whom he derided daily and forced to wear the shortest skirts and highest heels. And people phoned him. Important people were begging for a word in his ear.

It felt like what he should always have wanted. But after a few years, he realised that it was not.

Perhaps it was the city. Everything fitted together too well. His life was too neat. He woke up at five-thirty every morning, jogged for twenty-five minutes, jumped on a bus at six-thirty, after a light breakfast, arrived at work by seven, and stayed there until nine or ten at night, earning money. At first, this routine had been fulfilling, or at least its product had been, but it grew to feel pointless. His time was ticking away, and in pursuit of what? Money had stopped having any relevance to him. He liked having it, but he took it for granted now that it was plentiful.

As far as Peter was concerned, he worked those long hours solely to maintain the status quo.

The repetition, as much as anything, made him miserable; the dull thud of the days. And all the mod cons – the electric typewriter and the Newton's Cradle on his desk – were annoying tapping contraptions. The Thames Valley was too flat, the grass too short, and the stars – his childhood companions – forever shrouded by the city lights. Whether Peter liked it or not, he couldn't escape his past. His parents' lifestyle had been bred into his bones. Frequently, he felt uneasy about his choice of concrete over earth.

And so, Peter fled now and then to the mountains. An 'executive holiday' he termed it, but it was more than that: it was an acknowledgement of who he was and where he came from. He spent a few weeks each year hiking, basing himself in bed-and-breakfasts in small villages along the way. Up in the mountains, he watched the stars like dust, so plentiful that they seemed like an illusion. His cooking fire spat out fireflies that danced for a while in infinity before failing and turning into soot. Sometimes, he spotted comets, little scratches across the sky, which disappeared whenever he blinked. He thought often of his parents and the whirlwind that his life had become since their death.

Peter was twenty-five when he met Mary, a teacher in a hamlet in Snowdonia. It was magical to watch him talk about her years later when he and I sat together on the park bench in Cambridge. His eyes brightened, and his voice lowered.

'The moment I first saw her, I knew I had a twin.'

The memory of her breathed life into him. Blood, it seemed, was still pumping beneath his skin, warm as ever, albeit turned purple with regret. In memory, Mary was Peter's solace.

How they met, I don't know. All that concerns me is the time they spent together. Peter told me of countless dusks they spent watching day melt into night. Sunsets make me mourn now for a love long lost. I picture them scouring Mount Snowdon in search of the giant's tomb that's fabled to rest there. I watch them explore deep caves, concealed for centuries beneath scrub and twisted undergrowth, and wandering hand in hand like children amongst meadows of crickets, with sunshine pouring down on them like honey. Mary reintroduced magic to Peter's life. Their love existed in a lost world.

At some point, they married. Peter insisted that they set up a home back in London. His business could not survive long without him.

Peter was happier than he ever thought he deserved. Home was a retreat from the real world: the city. Productivity targets deadened his days; his wife's touch breathed life into his evenings. He could have survived like that. His life – and mine – could have been very different.

In 1979, Thatcher came to power, setting the economic tone for the eighties. Peter's business fell foul to market pressures and policies whose only purpose was to ruin him. It seemed to him that everyone was out to get him. His competitors were merciless. They pounced on his every mistake and offered no helping hand when he fell to his knees. Debt grew as an ache in the sinuses. Buyout offers came in from everywhere, insultingly low. Peter's failure was others' gain. His business, his dream, was at the mercy of scavengers.

He resisted, of course. He was a stubborn man at the best of times, but this was his parents' money he was losing now. Their deaths could not be in vain. Peter spent long nights in his office, with an angle-poise lamp beating down on his moist brow and whitening hair. The element fried his brain with its 100-watt intensity. He flicked through paper and toyed with figures, immersing himself in accounts. He had little choice but to take out a loan to keep the business afloat. He fought for contracts from the biggest airlines. He was determined that he would not lose. This spell of bad luck would not kill him. He was better than it.

The first thing Peter lost was his wife. He should have seen this coming – he gave nothing to her in those dark days. He returned home only to sleep and pick at the meals she prepared for him. Mary watched her husband wither away, painfully conscious of the fact that it was him that tied her to the accursed city. Mary longed for her village, her real home. As the years passed, she found less and less of Peter to cling to, less binding her to the life they both hated. In

1985, Mary filed for divorce. Shortly afterwards, Peter filed for bankruptcy.

Peter didn't know what to do or where to go. Mary had been his anchor, the one person who had reminded him that there was life away from the office. He knew he had pushed her away, but that had been necessary for the company's sake. Now, he had neither her nor the business that had destroyed them. Until then, happiness had seemed just around the corner, just a working week away, a contract won, or the prospect of a guilt-free hour or two with his wife. It had moved beyond the grasp of even blind optimism. Time existed only to grate at him.

Peter moved to Cambridge in the early 1990s. He rented a bedsit and took up manual labour to make ends meet. He was capable of more but could see no reason to make life better for himself, only for it to be taken away again. He wallowed in misery, and existence became a throbbing headache. Alcohol distorted time, and his memories were painful, blurred images.

Peter missed Mary still, but differently from before. She represented little now but intimacy. He missed her touch, her warmth, and the smoothness of her skin, but he had been alone for so long that these seemed like flashes from a past life. He no longer yearned for a union of spirits, that childish belief in one love, pure and ultimate. No, he just wanted flesh. Women were the only thing that captured his interest. He fantasised about girls he saw on the street, in supermarkets and on TV, imagining the taste of their sweat. He lay back on his stained bed and visualised them straddling him amongst the rotting food and clutter that covered every surface of his box room. The desire in him made every cell of his body quiver like molecules in heat. He made love to a fantasy with his hands until his body shuddered and jolted, spitting his essence over him. He despised himself and knew he was pathetic, but lust had wrapped around him, and he didn't have the strength to peel it away.

There was a church across the road from Peter's bedsit. He never told me which one, but it must have been near the town centre because students frequented it. He watched them every Sunday morning after coming around from alcohol-induced sleep. His head throbbed. He peered through net curtains, tarred yellow, sheltering his eyes from the sun.

The students came in groups. He learned later that this was because many met up at the Christian Union breakfasts they held in most colleges. The mix of characters intrigued Peter. He had always imagined young Christians falling into two categories: shy, freckled kids who talked to God because everybody else ignored them, or the choirboys on show every year on Carols from King's – pompous sods whose family's wealth had purchased them that privilege. Looking down at the churchgoers from his private hell, Peter was forced to revise his opinions. These people looked so normal, so regular, so healthy. He watched them because they were pure.

It was the girl's laugh that first caught his attention. It rippled above the whisper of the city and eased with the fresh morning air through the cracks in the window frame. Peter was used to hearing people outside – it was a busy street. He usually blocked out the noise subconsciously, but something about this laugh penetrated. It was soft and vibrant: beauty without art, music, or form.

Peter rolled out of bed, on which he had lain, eyes open, tracing outlines of spacecraft from indentations in the ceiling. He had been trying to get himself up for ages, to stare at people rather than plaster. Her laugh spurred him into action. He crawled through the rubbish to the window and pressed his face to the glass. It was too early in the morning for many people to be around, so it was easy to identify that laugh's owner. Two girls crossed the road to the church, one blonde, the other red-headed. He knew it was them. He could only see them from behind as they climbed the stairs to the oak door beneath the stained-glass window, but they both looked incredible. Especially the blond. Reality bowed to her – the rest of the scene wavered like colours through heat, but she was clear. The world was a backdrop to her.

Peter was no fool and no stranger to sex. He knew the hold it could have over people. Like everyone, he had seen it employed against him in advertising campaigns. He had posters on his walls, photographs of scantily clad women in provocative poses, images that simultaneously exulted and degraded them. Sex, to him, was mundane. He craved it still, but there was no mystery, no magic, just a biological compulsion. He felt something different that day, however. It wasn't lust that made his eyes follow those girls into the church. It was something more: it was gravity. Only later would Peter find a term that adequately described it, a term he used lightly and often when tutoring me, but there it was unmistakable; it physically pushed him.

God's will.

The minute the girls were gone, Peter rushed to the sink and tidied himself up. He tried to run a comb through his hair, which had matted and clumped together. He abandoned the implement (minus a few of its teeth) in favour of his fingers. He scraped a razor across his skin. Finally, he splashed water across his forehead and dabbed away the sweat beneath his armpits. Satisfied with his reflection in the toothpaste-splattered mirror, he kicked his way through the rubbish towards the front door.

For the first time in his life, Peter went to church.

* * *

Peter watched the girl from amongst the congregation. He did this Sunday after Sunday, week after week. For months, she was the centre of his world. She sat with her friend. She listened closely to sermons and stood when instructed to put her soul into singing. She had no reason to notice Peter, who watched her from a few rows behind. So powerful was his infatuation, and so crippling was the ice that spread under his skin whenever he saw her that he could do nothing but stare.

One time, he overheard another student talk to her. He called her 'Helen'.

Helen. If ever there was a name worthy of that girl, it was Helen, the face that launched a thousand ships. Peter felt closer to her than ever, with her name in his possession.

Peter constructed a complete three-dimensional image of Helen before they even spoke. She was unlike all the other girls he had ever known. No make-up and none of the sexuality he had come to associate with the objects he now desired, yet she seemed confident and at ease with herself in how she moved and talked. She was plain, robust pretty, with rich dark eyes, glowing skin and clothes that didn't exhibit but weren't too functional either... they were just right. She flowed; that was how he described it. Everything she did was natural. This was what made her stand out. Peter had become unaccustomed to equating self-confidence with anything other than wealth and sex appeal.

Peter also developed a fixed idea of what Helen wanted – what she would accept – and it was evident to him that only a Christian would do. The moment he saw Helen enter the church that day, Christianity became something he craved, an entrance ticket into an exclusive club that contained her. So, he studied, beginning with the Gospels. Christ was the way in.

Peter aimed for comprehensive knowledge of the divine, hoping that it would conceal his ungodly ways. His studies were a means to an end, but the word of God held power. It tugged at him as he read. Christ knew him and had seen his faults two thousand years earlier when roaming the earth as a man. Peter wasn't reading to believe nor even to understand, but Christ's every word held relevance, and every parable struck home. Peter was one of the lost sheep Christ spoke of in Luke: a sinner whose repentance would be celebrated by 'rejoicing in the presence of the angels of God'. He loved the idea of people rejoicing about him.

The preachers' spirited sermons stung him, too. They nudged him towards faith just as much as Christ – and Helen – coaxed. He edged so close to it that the world seemed unreal. The foundation stone upon which he had built his knowledge – the belief that cold, hard science could explain everything – got knocked away. Every image wavered, and every object bowed to a greater authority. He saw death and decay everywhere, and he feared damnation.

Although he knew in his heart that it was wrong, Peter continued to pursue Helen. He put off attempts to speak to her for the first few weeks. He was rusty when it came to the fundamentals of human interaction. But he gained confidence as he cleaned himself up, washed and shaved properly, bought new clothes, and poured alcohol in his flat down the sink. He started to feel like a person again, not just an animal pursuing its desires.

Peter turned then to practicalities. Helen was popular and, as such, was never alone. That red-haired friend of hers stayed with her most of the time. Peter grew to resent her.

On those rare occasions when she failed to show, he tried to move in for the kill, but somebody else always got there first. Just about every male in the church vied for the prize of a single unbridled conversation, an opportunity to stand out from the crowd. Helen handled this well, aware that she had unwittingly nurtured affection and that this burdened her with a duty as a landmark in other people's lives. She was modest and gentle when deflecting advances, never too full of herself or, crucially, too interested in any of the boys. Still, this didn't bring Peter any closer to making contact.

It happened finally by accident at one of the lunches the church held after the service. Peter had taken to staying behind, less now because of Helen, more to talk to her fellow Christians. They were friendly enough: plain, introverted sorts, quite often devoid of humour but strong in faith. He knew that he could benefit from their company by immersing himself in their world.

That day was the first time Peter ever prayed (a fact that underpinned his interpretation of what followed). He remained seated as the others filed down the stairs to the hall where lunch was served. Head bowed, he considered the service that had just passed and the feeling that had risen in his stomach as he raised his voice in praise of God. He felt hopeful now. Whether or not he came to know Helen, this experience had bettered him, opening his heart again to the possibility of a world full of love. He clasped his hands together and whispered under his breath.

'I don't know if you're out there, but if you are, please hear me. I want to believe. I want you to guide me.'

Peter loitered there a while, thinking. He was so late going to lunch that all the chairs had been filled. One table made space for him. It was Helen's.

Helen introduced herself, and they shook hands as

strangers. Peter joined her and four others in prayer as a simple meal was laid out for them: bread, stew and dumplings. The students all knew each other but didn't treat Peter as an outsider. He had never really had friends, and he realised what he had been missing in such company. They were so free and forthcoming in how they spoke to each other, so warm and trusting. Sharing food and faith, he was one of them, part of a community.

But it was a lie. Had they known the life Peter had lived and the things he had done, they would have been horrified. They couldn't bond with someone who had lost as he had. They couldn't accept the decisions he had made. Their lives still held promise; they still had a future. He had nothing left to give. But they didn't need to know that.

Peter told them he was a mature student and a seeker of truth. This new character had given up a successful career in media, believing there was something more to all this. These untruths opened doors. Helen invited him back to her college room to talk about God. This became a regular fixture every Sunday after church. They sat together, sharing herbal tea, squinting in the sunlight that streamed in through the tall, warm windows, attaching to her. He was with her alone, and that in itself made him very happy. All they did was talk.

Finding Christ had been easy for Helen. She was born into a Christian family, so the divine was as real to her as the air she breathed and the ground she trod. Her parents had introduced her to a Christ as unequivocal in existence as the fact that a tree is a tree, and a table a table. But she understood Peter's situation, or, at least, professed to. She told him about the ups and downs of her relationship with Jesus: the tragedies that had caused her to question her faith, and how Christ had always shone through and was always there for her. Peter, in turn, shared everything with her. He forgot that half of it was lies. So convincing was his new persona that he talked himself into believing it. As this Peter spent time with Helen, he discovered an intimacy greater than physical attraction and unparalleled even by the wispy myth-driven romance he had shared with his wife.

It was not fated to last. As the seasons passed, Peter became conscious of the barrier between them. Helen would divulge plenty about her past but nothing about her present. Thus far and no further, she just wouldn't let him in. This frustrated him terribly: it was all very well knowing how she'd got where she was, but he wanted to know her now and how she filled the days. The problem, he realised, was faith. He was still a seeker. How could she form any kind of attachment to him when, as far as she was concerned, he was damned? She was a child of God – Christ would save her; Peter had only doubt and oblivion, the tortuous depths of Hell. Not even love could cross that divide. They lived in different worlds, and they would have very different fates.

So that was it. Peter had to have faith. He tried and tried, battering at the structure of his mind, the ballasts that held it in place until, finally, something gave way.

It happened in the public toilets on the corner of Parker's Piece. Peter had walked there every night for the past three weeks, straight through the park, ignoring the giggles of young couples in the darkness, the ramblings of the dispossessed and the groans of chronic gamblers lying bruised in the mud; weeping and gnashing of teeth. The toilet block should have been locked, but kids had forced their way in before being driven away by the stench of stale urine.

He went there to be alone with his thoughts, to find a peace that eluded him in his bedsit, which overlooked the church and all its memories.

Peter locked the door to the cubicle and sat down. He gripped his chin and ground his teeth. How he wanted her! Everything about her drew him in: her eyes, her smile, her spirit. She was trying to save him from his worldly life and share God's love. How he wanted that! He longed for her to take his hand and lead him into a paradise, warm and bright and full of summer days, devoid of past.

He sighed a quivering breath and felt the heat slip through his fingers. All he lacked was faith. How desperately he needed to be saved, but he could only believe in what he could see.

How could he possibly rationalise it? He had been struggling with this for weeks, approaching it from every angle, trying to find the first rung of a ladder that led, direct and certain, to God. Whichever way he looked at it, he had to start with faith. Every argument for God had ten against, all of which could be dismissed with the simple comeback, 'That may be your opinion, but I believe in something greater.' Faith was a trump card. But he could only attain it by plunging into an abyss, at the bottom of which lay either revelation or delusion; he was not sure which.

He had to wrestle down his doubts. He had to pin them down and spit on them. This wasn't science. It couldn't be proven. He had to set aside the part of him that required proof.

Peter hadn't slept properly for weeks. He felt like crying all the time, just breaking down and sobbing uncontrollably. The world was a dream. Reality wavered to such an extent that he wondered if the bonds between particles might loosen and objects turn to putty. If he were to lay his hand on the cubicle door and push just hard enough, might skin and bone pass through chipboard and graffiti?

He paused, hand outstretched, shaking. That was it! His struggle at last was over. It struck him that he couldn't see the particles that made up the objects around him, but he believed in them, just as he believed in some invisible force binding them together as solids. He couldn't see anything beyond the cubicle, but he knew the sinks were there, with taps fastened into place by scum and lime scale. And he couldn't see the girl he longed for, but she was always with him, an after-image stencilled onto everything. Where did knowledge end and faith begin? Perhaps the two were not as irreconcilable as he thought.

Besides, there was so much that he accepted but didn't fully understand. He couldn't begin to fathom how the human body worked or how electrical signals in his brain translated into consciousness. Why not add something else to that list? God could explain them all, could tie them all together.

If he listened hard, could he hear His voice?

Peter could feel his weary mind giving way. Faith structured it now, introducing its filing system. Lust and lies were cast as sin, and sections of his brain were marked 'Out of Bounds.' As a Christian, he would have no cause to access them again. His thoughts restructured queries to be resolved with reference to God, everything to revolve around Him.

But it wasn't God he adored.

Peter could feel his shackles now, as solid as the forbidden zones in his mind. He would wear them for the rest of his life. As he followed the light, door after door banged closed behind him, locking his identity away with his sins. The door at the end of the corridor stood ajar, bleeding light into the darkness of his mind. When he pushed it open and stepped through, only one scenario remained that made any sense.

He believed.

# Chapter 14

## *Rejoice!*

It was Christmas Eve. Mum and I were on our way to midnight mass at St Mary's, the 'tourist church' next to the Market Square. We were running late, so we parked outside King's College, risking a ticket. We hurried down King's Parade and entered King's College Chapel, paying scant attention to the traffic cones that adorned its spires, placed there by reckless students. The vicar must have been wearing thermal underwear, standing in the doorway, greeting everyone. They had set out portable heaters in force inside the church, but drafts of cold air swept around my ankles as we took our seats.

Frostbite concerns aside, I enjoyed the service. I hadn't been to midnight mass before, on account of my childhood strategy of hurrying in Christmas morning (and its presents) with an early night. Peter had persuaded me to stay up this time to 'welcome Christ's coming with worship'. Mum insisted on accompanying me. I think she saw it as a potential bonding activity.

So, it transpired that she and I sat at one end of a pew, and Peter took up residence across the aisle. There I was, straddling two worlds, Mum to my left and Peter to my right.

Fortunately, Mum didn't pick up on any familiarity between us. She glanced questioningly at Peter several times, but only during the hymns. I put this down to his voice. He wasn't the greatest of singers, but he didn't allow this to temper his fervour. He pushed his voice too far, producing a flat, penetrating wail. *'Oh come all ye faithful, joyful and tuneless!'*

Fortunately, too, Peter didn't say anything to Mum. I had been worried that he would start ranting on at her about how she had taught me only ungodly ways and had failed in her duties as a mother. But he was silent and careful to acknowledge me only with a discreet glance. Apparently, he did recognise some cultural necessities. Our relationship was not one to be advertised.

It was a nice service, anyway. It felt how Christmases should feel. Proper *Miracle on 34<sup>th</sup> Street* stuff: traditional carols, rosy-cheeked singers still wearing their scarves; just a general sense of joy. There was a wreath on the door and candles everywhere, flames shivering. I could tell the atmosphere was affecting Mum – she kept putting her arm around me and pulling me close. Everybody was being unnaturally nice to each other, smiling at complete strangers. It was as though we had stepped back to an era when there was trust, civility, and community; we were all 'companions on this great expedition called life' (to quote my grandfather's phrase, which he had probably borrowed from somebody else).

If anything, Peter seemed ill at ease with it all. It didn't take a great deal of imagination for me to work out what he was thinking: that this was all just trimming; there was no substance to any of it. People sang carols because of traditions. They sang them because they liked the tunes, and they conjured images of years past. Who among them believed passionately in their message? And I could see him eyeing up the models in the nativity scene, assessing how cheap they looked. Did they have 'Made in Taiwan' printed on their bases? Mass-produced trash, unfit for the house of God.

To be honest, I didn't care what he thought about any of this. This was *my* Christmas. I *wanted* it over-the-top and stylised.

Who was I trying to fool? This was never going to be a proper family Christmas. Not the way things were.

Christmas Day was a sombre affair. Mum and I had a present each: she got me a computer game, and I got her chocolates. We bought them together a couple of days earlier, in theory for mutual support, but in practice to eradicate every last bit of fun from proceedings. We were going through the motions. I don't know why we bothered to wrap the presents at all.

I did get something from my father: a ten-pound note in an envelope. He was never one for frills, my father.

Actually, that was the first time I really missed him. My father used to be great on special occasions: he made an effort and got you into the swing of things. He was a lot more extroverted (a.k.a. hot-headed) than me and Mum, and he didn't hold back. At Christmas, he sang carols all day and insisted on us joining in. He wouldn't let us tuck into dinner until he was satisfied that we had overcome any inhibitions we might have had. And he used to make me play football in the garden afterwards, even if there were two feet of snow on the ground. That was the only time of year we ever kicked that football. I only did it because he forced me to. I missed that. And the way he used to ruffle my hair afterwards, like I was five years old, I missed that too. One thing to be said about my father: if you weren't having a good time, he'd harangue you until you did. Fun. Threatening but fun.

That Christmas, Mum and I ate junk food and watched TV. We didn't talk except to ask each other to change the channel or pass the cheese straws. Not far removed from what the majority of the nation got up to, I'll wager, but it was nothing compared to what I was used to. I went upstairs and played on the computer for a while. Mum didn't complain. It was Christmas Day, and she didn't even nag me about shutting myself away in my room. Something was badly amiss.

By evening, I was back down on the settee. I hadn't missed much – Mum had watched *White Christmas*. We sat together through a BBC adaptation of *David Copperfield*, turning over at nine to watch the *Touch of Frost* Christmas special.

'I'm off to bed,' I said to Mum once Frost had nailed the killer.

As I got up, I knocked an empty box of Turkish Delight onto the floor. The icing sugar puffed up like a toxic cloud.

'Okay, love,' Mum said, flicking through the channels. 'See you in the morning.'

I was almost through the door when Mum said, 'Happy Christmas.'

I turned around. Our eyes met for the first time that day. So that was that. That was our Christmas.

'Happy Christmas,' I said.

I couldn't focus my thoughts enough to pray that night, so I just recited the Lord's Prayer and hoped that would cover me.

Half an hour later, I heard Mum brushing her teeth.

Then, the landing light went off. In the final minutes before midnight, all that was left of Christmas was the click of the house cooling and the churn of my stomach.

* * *

New Year's Eve was a bit more raucous. I went to my first-ever New Year's party. Jo invited me during one of those detentions we spent together.

'You want to spend New Year with me?' she wrote on a scrap of paper. 'There's this gathering I'm going to.'

I studied that note for quite a while, wondering what exactly I was supposed to read into it. I wouldn't have pondered it so much if she'd written something like, '*I'm going to a party. Want to come?*' or, '*Are you going to the party?*' Those questions contained no subtext; there was no '*with me*' in them. By contrast, the central proposition of her statement was that we spend time together. The party was incidental, wasn't it?

No doubt about it, the sensible answer was 'Yes'. But how was it customary to react? I didn't want Jo to think I was jumping to conclusions and assuming this was some kind of... date.

'What's happening exactly?' I replied.

'Some friends of mine are getting together for a bit of a bash.'

It turned out that 'some friends' translated as Jo's entire year group and that the term 'bash' was to be taken literally. Hardly surprising, considering that the hostess was Joyce MacLachlan, whose gatherings were legendary. You knew about it when there was a MacLachlan party going on. Rumours spread around the school like head lice: excited whispers of drink, drugs and rave music. The hospital cleared its beds, and everyone put 999 on speed dial. Police, fire, ambulance, all the emergency services had been called out to a MacLachlan party at one time or another. I'm told they even had to send cave rescue on one occasion. There were tales of attendees going missing and regaining consciousness days later in the Peak District with only an umbrella, a *Happy Meal* toy, and half a bag of *Jelly Babies* to their name.

Her parents didn't exactly calm things down. No, they were always in the thick of it. They had a reputation for getting trolleyed and attempting to incite an orgy.

I suspected that these tales were grossly exaggerated, but this didn't stop my hands from shaking as I got ready. I had real difficulty with my shirt buttons. Something big and nasty was about to happen. I dug the smartest smart-casual shirt I owned out of the corner of my wardrobe, hoping it would help me fit in. It wasn't enough: even scrubbed up and drowned in aftershave, I knew I was way out of my depth. Wasn't I supposed to hate parties?

I hadn't forgotten, either, that I was *persona non-gratis* among certain elements of my year group. Punching your school's head boy tends to do that to you.

'How well do you know Joyce?' I asked Jo as we walked there. We were carrying a couple of bags of alcopops, which her parents had bought for her from the off-license.

'Not at all, really,' Jo said. 'Mainly my parents, they know hers. They do quiz nights together – tour the pubs, and pretty much make quite a living out of it. Who'd have thought watching TV and soaking up trivia could be so profitable? I'm not going because of Joyce. Pretty much no one is.'

'What's wrong with her?'

Jo rolled her eyes and said, 'It's New Year's Eve. A party's a party.'

It descended on me, then, the ordeal that lay ahead of me.

'This isn't going to be awful, is it?'

Jo regarded me as though I had just spoken in a foreign language. 'I can't believe you're thinking like that when we've got these.'

She raised her bag of drinks and grinned.

It *was* awful. Diabolically so. It was basically just like every other party I had ever been to, only that bit more over-crowded. An added element of danger spiced up the atmosphere, but that wasn't really what I looked for in a night out.

Joyce's place seemed built for demolition. The walls were stripped of paper, the floors of carpets. Half of the furniture had been cleared, and the other half was covered with polythene. The MacLachlans were in the middle of redecorating. I couldn't help but feel it was a bad move inviting people into this. You know what they say about vandalism: leave one window broken, and there'll be five within a week. The same applied there. There was nothing there to tiptoe around, nothing to respect. What transpired was inevitable: the hall filled with smokers, who proceeded to drop cigarette butts, crisp packets and empty cans all over the place. Some guests took it upon themselves to contribute their modern art ideas to the decor, splashing drinks up the walls or bleeding onto the floor. You could get away with anything there.

The mood wasn't helped much by the gangster rap they were playing, offensively loud. So many expletives that I felt faint. It set the scene for turf war down in the ghetto. Early on, I noticed gangs form: those sporting red items of clothing, cap-wearers, those with facial hair and those without. Iron gazes met. It was ridiculous, watching this in the middle of Cambridge. *West Side Story* seemed grittier than ever before.

I hid at the top of the stairs for the first few hours, looking miserable. This was the only place I could find where I could sit without getting kicked. The drawback was that I repeatedly had to make way for couples going to and from the bedrooms.

I had a fair idea of what they were doing in there. Had the music not been so loud, I would probably have heard it, too. But did they have to flaunt it in my face like that? At one point, a couple headed for one of the vacant rooms. The bloke started to undo his jeans halfway up the stairs. The worst bit was when I went looking for the bathroom. I had to choose the wrong door, didn't I? I was confronted by a view of this woman wearing only bunny ears, preparing to give Mr Spader (the youngest teacher in school, fresh from training) the time of his life. This was my Biology teacher! From then on, I turned red whenever he mentioned reproduction (even of fruit flies), and I pitied the rabbits they kept in the science labs.

Later, Mr and Mrs MacLachlan pushed their way past; he a caricature of a man, with a face that drooped like a wax sculpture in sunlight, and she a tangle of flesh and leather. He winked at me as they passed. She giggled.

I might have felt better about it had I been getting some action, too. I was supposed to be at this thing with Jo, but I didn't have a clue where she'd gone. One moment, she had been pushing her way into the kitchen, promising to get me a drink; the next thing I knew, I was abandoned to my fate. An hour or so later, I caught sight of her with some girl-friends. She seemed to have forgotten all about me. Later, she was with this guy who looked very interested in her. He didn't seem able to keep his hands to himself. She didn't seem to mind, either – she talked quite freely with him while he was groping her. I decided to leave them to it.

Sam, Michael and Brian hadn't, of course, been invited. I say, 'of course', but it *was* a bit of a surprise that Sam wasn't there. This must have been too low-brow for him. My friends were probably all having nights in with their families.

After a while, I realised I was pretty thirsty. I headed down the stairs to get myself another can of lemonade. This became an epic quest. A group of students stood halfway down, engaged in intense debate about existentialism (although I didn't once hear any of them pronounce it correctly). They didn't move for me or notice I was there, even when I coughed and tapped one of them on the shoulder. In the end, I had to mount the bannister and shimmy down. Another guy had fallen asleep on the bottom step. I leapt over him and landed on this girl, knocking her drink down her dress. An anxious moment ensued as she looked down at herself before realising it wouldn't stain because she had been drinking white wine, not red. She hiccupped, and I was on my way.

My God, the noise! So many people shouting at each other over the music. There were no soft furnishings to absorb any of the racket. And the heat, all those bodies packed tight. Everywhere I looked, there was an elbow or set of pecks two inches from my face. In every corner, young people were smoking themselves older. I felt like gagging. The air had the consistency of *Sunny Delight*. The front door was open, but this didn't seem to have had much effect. I could see just as many people in the gravel front garden and on the street as inside.

I didn't get much further before a familiar face appeared from nowhere: Natalie Powell, girlfriend of Sean, the guy whose nose I had had a fair go at breaking. This wasn't good. She had spotted me and was heading in my direction with this determined expression on her face. The starkness of her make-up – her green eye shadow throwing into relief her red hair – served, for some reason, to make her seem all the more intimidating. I couldn't see Sean anywhere – that was some relief – but Natalie was still a force to be reckoned with. I had her down as one of the active conspirators in the campaign against Brian.

There was no getting away from her. She was a force that could part crowds; I was a non-entity that nobody could be fussed to look at, never mind make way for.

'What's your name?' Natalie shouted to me.

'Um,' I said. 'Nick. Nick Farlowe.' I looked down at the ground as a peasant might do before his lord.

'Listen,' she said. 'I just wanted to say, "Good on you" for the other week.'

I blinked at her.

'Me and Sean aren't together anymore. Two-timing bastard! Hasn't got it, you know, where you need it, and thinks he can make up for it by sleeping around.'

'Um.'

She threw her arms around me and did one of those air kisses (almost), smudging my cheek with lipstick. I don't think it was supposed to be such a spectacular gesture: the alcohol had a say in that.

That was the first time a girl ever hugged me. I closed my eyes and endured it. It wasn't too bad. She felt nice. Not my type at all, though. Smelt too much of cigarettes.

'Thank you,' I said when she withdrew.

'No, thank *you*.' Natalie pointed a finger vaguely in my direction.

Just then, someone called to her, and she was gone.

I took a moment to steady myself, but it was no good. I could feel people looking at me, weighing me up. What did they see? Actually, I didn't want to know. I was well aware that I was nothing to them. They were colourful and confident and loud; I was a pathetic stereotype whose emotional depth was masked by his murmur of a voice, his overlarge forehead, and the people he spent his time with. Being in that place brought it all back, all my embarrassments. All those stupid things I'd said and done over the years were visible to everyone.

I realised, quite calmly and mechanically, that spots were appearing in front of my eyes. My brain had begun to slow. What was this? I had been drinking from cans all night; there was no way my drink had been spiked. So why was I standing in the middle of a motorway with cars whizzing past around me? My breaths had turned short and swift, and my heart was pounding like anything.

I had to find Jo and tell her I was leaving. That was the best thing.

Then, I had to get out of there.

I needed air. It couldn't wait any longer.

I ended up in the back garden. It was a mud pit. No one else seemed willing to risk ruining their shoes, so I was alone. I stretched my arms wide. It was pitch black out there, virtue of the fir trees, which blotted out the moon. It was a fair-sized garden. I could make out images of what appeared to be statuettes lingering on the edge of darkness. As I moved away from the house, I realised that these were parts of a bathroom set. I pictured this scene as an exhibit in the Tate Modern. From the smell, I judged that somebody had made use of the toilet before realising that it wasn't plumbed in. Interactive art.

I wandered deeper into the surreal land of *Royal Doulton*. The racket from indoors was less immediate there, but there was still no escaping it. My head was buzzing. But at least I could breathe again.

It wasn't long before someone joined me out there in the wilderness. I saw them come out, silhouetted against the house. It took quite a while for me to realise it was Jo. Her profile looked quite different out there. I noticed things I hadn't seen before: how skinny she was, how big her hoop earrings were, and how she strutted clumsily on those heels. And as my eyes adjusted, I noticed the drained colour of her hair, and the makeup she had pasted on during a raid on her sister's vanity case. She wasn't any better or worse like this, just different.

I started smiling despite myself.

Jo still hadn't seen me. I'm not sure if she would have done had it been broad daylight – the way she was walking suggested she'd drunk a few too many of those alcopops. I kept my distance, still mad at her for abandoning me.

So, why the smile? It started when Jo began vomiting into the bathtub. It felt good to know that her actions had consequences.

I'm not sure what happened next. The next thing I knew, I had stepped out of the darkness, leaned forward and pulled the hair back from Jo's face. What was going on? Evidently, I felt more comfortable dealing with bodily functions than conversation. Or was it chivalry? Had my mother's efforts to bring me up properly finally taken effect?

'Having a good time?' Jo said, between bouts of emptying her stomach.

'Yeah,' I said. 'You?'

'I'm good,' she said. She then tilted her head forward and spewed into the bath again.

The stench of alcohol and digestive juices was so sharp that my stomach turned. Most disgusting of all was the body heat emanating from the bathtub.

'Where have you been?' Jo asked.

'I could ask you the same question.'

Jo's eyes grew distant as she delved into memory. 'Where *have* I been?' she asked herself. Then: 'Oh, God!'

She began to retch like a cat about to cough up a fur ball.

I felt myself gag, so I turned my head away until she had finished.

'What the hell was I doing with that guy?' Jo said, wiping her mouth on her wrist.

'Practising your feminine wiles, as I recall.'

'That was before I got to the vomiting stage, was it?'

I nodded.

Jo looked at me for a while. 'I'm so sorry.'

I shrugged.

Proceedings were interrupted then by another bout of retching.

'What's the time?' Jo asked when she had recovered.

I pressed the glow-light button on my watch.

'Eleven fifty-seven.' I hadn't realised it was so late.

'I think I've had a bit much to drink.'

'Maybe.'

Jo's manner changed suddenly:

'You're laughing at me, aren't you? You think you're better than me because you haven't touched a drop in your life. You don't know a bloody...'

She turned and vomited again.

It struck me then that the time we live through is the

only thing that unifies everyone in the world. Midnight was descending on us like a tidal wave. Sooner or later, everyone would pass through that pivotal moment when one millennium would end, and another (clean, fresh and new, unsullied by human error) would begin. New Year seemed like a great leveller: however you lived it, you couldn't avoid it. Families were spending it together, couples were about to share a glass of wine, friends were priming bottles of champagne, celebrities were snorting cocaine or getting wasted at some exclusive party, and couch potatoes watched *Goodbye to the Nineties* (reliving a decade spent on that same spot on the sofa). For a fraction of time, the world made sense. Everybody fitted into their niche, and by that, they could be judged.

When the countdown started in Joyce McLachlan's house, I was outside in the cold, trying my best to stop vomit from getting into the hair of a girl who had ditched me in favour of company she could barely remember. How telling was that? More telling, perhaps, was that I was happy.

New Year's gatherings have never done it for me, even to this day. They're always a disappointment, with everyone trying too hard to be ecstatic. This party was a little different because hardly anyone knew where they were, never mind what century it was, but I'm not sure this made it any better. Countdowns I've been to since then were advertised as a kind of salve, an opportunity to mark an end to a year of troubles, to compartmentalise the bad parts of your life. The turn of the year 2000 could have been like that for me. I had every reason to want to bid farewell to the past few months. And to adolescence, for that matter.

Life never works out like that.

Big Ben struck. Everyone cheered. Party poppers fired.

Across the country, a million corks flew. As they fell to earth like hailstones, I realised that nothing had changed.

After a while, Jo groaned and raised herself to her feet.

'What's the time?' she asked.

'Twelve o'clock,' I said. 'Happy New Year.'

She grabbed me then without warning and made to kiss me. I managed to slip free.

'What's the matter?'' she demanded as I turned my face away.

I pointed to the area around my mouth.

'Oh.'

Jo sat back dejectedly on the rim of the bathtub. She reached into her pocket for a tissue. I volunteered to get her some water.

'Thank you,' she said without looking at me.

The moment had definitely passed.

# Chapter 15

## *Ensnared*

A few days later, I got a letter from Jo. She had posted it first class. The envelope was pink and bore a seasonal stamp with a robin on it. It was quite exciting. I didn't often receive letters. Especially pink ones.

I went up to my room to open it. I already had a fair idea who it was from, on account of the handwriting, which I recognised from the notes Jo had passed me in detention. Besides, I only knew so many girls, and I couldn't imagine any of my male friends sending me something that looked like that.

I made sure that the door was closed before ripping through the envelope. This turned out to be a wise move since the whiff of perfume that flooded out was potent enough to fell anyone in the vicinity. Jo must have literally marinated the paper in it; it was that strong. The scent was familiar: fruit – bark and berries, with a hint of... I'll stop there before I sound too much like a wine taster. Anyway, it was definitely Jo's. I hadn't consciously noticed it on her before, but the association was there in my brain, sufficient to conjure the illusion that she was there in the room with me.

I sat down on my bed and unfolded the paper, pink too, with a *Winnie the Pooh* illustration in the corner.

The letter was written strangely. I still have it – it's hard to throw stuff like that away. I dug it out when I was visiting Mum. It just smells of paper now.

'Dear Nick,' it read. 'Thanks for New Year. I had a great time. I just want to say I'm sorry about the thing. I woke up with one hell of a hangover, if that's any consolation. Hope you got home okay.'

Jo went on to spill her insides, relating various ordeals she had suffered over the years. I wasn't sure how any of it was relevant, but it was interesting, like *Oprah Winfrey*, only less scandalous. I wondered what she was trying to achieve by emulating those 'getting to know you' conversations that, for some reason, are obligatory during dates, when you regale your partner with details of family traumas and the gory bits of previous relationships. Somehow, crap like that is supposed to bring people together.

The final section of Jo's letter appeared to operate on the assumption that the preceding paragraphs had lowered my defences. She moved in for the kill, making it clear that it would be an excellent idea for me to go to hers sometime and help her out with maths. Given that we were still on Christmas holiday, and she was only just starting her GCSEs, it seemed obvious that she had no pressing need for revision. Other agendas were at play.

But what about how she acted at New Year's, practically ignoring me half the night? How did that fit in?

Conflicting messages aside, Jo had drawn me in. This was uncharted territory, and of course there were dangers, but I accepted them willingly. I touched the letter against my upper lip and breathed in deeply.

* * *

For the next few days, Jo was all I thought about. I kept drifting into a daze, revelling in this new-found sensation that someone might actually like me. It was a bit of a distraction. Everything else I did seemed dull and insignificant compared with the thought of being with her. The life I led seemed crappier than ever before, and my other interests seemed merely ways to pass the time until I would see her again.

I started to care about my appearance. That was a pain. What I wore had never really been a consideration before. My usual tactic of choosing the cheapest available garment no longer seemed so sensible. I needed a whole new wardrobe. My belly disgusted me, too; my general physique. Where were the muscles? I needed dumbbells, essential for any aspiring stud.

This whole situation was unprecedented. The idea that a girl might possibly be interested in me was equally appealing and frightening. What kind of psycho was she? And what exactly did she want from me? More importantly, what was I supposed to do about it?

There were only a few days left before we went back to school, and my friends had decided to squeeze in a *Warhammer* campaign. My elves were besieged by the combined forces of Sam's undead, Michael's dwarfs and Brian's goblins. My only line of defence was a shallow river and a matchstick fort. I felt more than a little victimised.

It confused them when I showed no signs of caring as my forces got slaughtered. Several times, Sam said, 'Sorry,

Nick, there goes another one of your heroes' and 'Whoops, a massacre!', but I just smiled and continued rolling dice. Later, Michael interrogated me about narcotic substances. There was definitely an element of concern to his questions. Perhaps he was worried about the potential influence of the *Bob Marley* tape he had lent me the week before.

But seriously, though, my perceptions *had* changed. Everywhere I looked, there were people who'd had sex: young mothers with pushchairs; older women with grainy skin from frolicking in meadows in the summers of their youth. On the drive back from Sam's (Mum picked me up), we stopped at a pedestrian crossing, and I felt like a customer in a peep show: girls strutted their stuff across the road like it was a catwalk. I knew I shouldn't have stared – Jo alone should have been my object of interest – but something inside me had been awakened. All those relationships I'd read about or seen on TV, that could be me – I was a sexual being, too.

Try though I might, I couldn't escape from those thoughts, and to be honest, they were doing my head in. I had to get away from them. One day, I cycled out past Girton, right into the countryside. The winter sky was cloudless, opaque. Hardy birds chattered in the still, leafless trees. I rode down deserted roads, passing farmhouses, retirement bungalows and miles of barren fields. I wanted the world to drop away so that I could catch a glimpse of transcendence, as I had done by the river that time. When would I be free of this surge of hungry thoughts? When would I be able to remember what drew me to Peter, and the greater truth I strove for before this carnal yearning began in earnest? I needed to remind myself who I was. But I couldn't escape the urban. It clung to me in the clothes I wore, the deodorant that clogged my pores, and the shower gel I had rubbed into my skin. For some reason, a *Culture Club* song I hadn't heard in years decided to switch itself on, blaring in my head, the same chorus over and over. Transcendence seemed far, far off.

Maybe I should have stuck less fixedly to the roads, which threaded their way through hamlets and cultivation. Just when I thought I was escaping from Cambridge, a car would overtake me, or a fellow cyclist would call 'hello' loudly as they passed. There's no such thing as countryside in England anymore. Somebody owns every patch of soil; it's always someone's back garden. The motor vehicle has made true isolation, too, a thing of the past. A lay-by, seemingly in the middle of nowhere, was strewn with litter: *McDonalds* takeaway packing (some new, some faded), cigarette butts, broken glass and empty cans of *Budweiser*. A shredded condom packet lay beside pieces of women's underwear, encrusted with dirt. My imagination ran wild.

I shook myself and looked away from those souvenirs. I turned my bike around and headed home. This was doing me no good whatsoever.

* * *

It wasn't until we went back to school that anything developed between Jo and me, and even then, it didn't happen immediately. The first chess club was excruciating – we didn't play each other or even talk. Instead, we followed Brian around, commenting on other people's games and making ourselves just as unpopular as him. Occasionally, we exchanged knowing glances when somebody made a particularly bad move, but that was the extent of our communication.

Did Jo want me to thank her for her letter or pretend

that I had never received it? The ball was squarely in my court. It was loaded with sidespin, and to top it all, one of my racquet strings had snapped (not that I want to stretch a metaphor). It was much easier when Jo was making the advances. My forte was response. I couldn't take the initiative and talk to her; I just couldn't.

I decided that day that I would write a reply to Jo's letter. I would tell her exactly how I felt. Surely, it had to be easier to put things down on paper than talk to her. I fancied myself as pretty good with words when I had the chance to consider them thoroughly. This was going to be easy.

It wasn't.

The first problem I encountered was a deficit of suitable writing paper. Everything in my room was crap – spiral notepads, pages torn out of schoolbooks – and I didn't have the disposable income to just go and buy paper *willy-nilly*. I had to settle for printer paper cut into A5 sheets, but it looked cheap.

Not a good start.

Next was the writing itself. My handwriting has always been terrible. Jo wouldn't have understood a word if I'd have gone ahead and poured my heart out without giving some thought to the lettering. I knew how to use a fountain pen – that was an option – but I didn't want my letter looking too flowery. I ended up printing everything in block capitals. The thing looked more like a shopping list than a love letter.

When I came around to thinking of something to write, I stumbled across the fundamental flaw in the whole plan: I didn't have a clue what the hell I wanted to say. How could I tell Jo about my true feelings when I didn't really know what these were? And how to start? *'I am writing to enquire whether you would consider union with me on a girlfriend-*

*boyfriend basis. Please indicate your consent by completing the enclosed reply slip and returning it to me at your earliest convenience.'*

Was I supposed to talk about her body parts – you know, their various merits? Honesty is everything in a relationship, but wouldn't that be too much too soon?

By the time I crawled into bed that night, the litter bin was overflowing, and I had nothing anywhere near useable to show for it.

Thankfully, matters were taken out of my hands the following day when I ran into Jo on my way home from school. She was sitting on a garden wall with her face in her hands, weeping exaggeratedly. This brought to the fore a gallant part of me. I tiptoed up, prodded her on the shoulder (hesitant about even that little body contact), and asked her what was the matter.

Jo lowered her hands and looked at me with those big blue eyes of hers. Her sobs ceased immediately, and I could see no trace of tears, but I didn't care.

'Maths,' she told me. 'I'd forgotten how bad it was. Christmas was great – I could forget about it for a while – but it's been waiting to pounce on me. I just...'

'Don't worry about it,' I said. 'I can, um, I can help you with it if you like.'

Jo caught a breath. 'You'd do that for me?'

'Sure.'

'That's so sweet of you!' Jo exclaimed, leaping up and flinging her arms around my neck. 'Friday night, my place?'

I gulped. 'Okay.'

'Great,' she said.

Seconds later, Jo had waved goodbye and was halfway down the street.

I stood there, blinking. Jo was well out of earshot when it dawned on me that this road wasn't on her route home.

But still, on Friday, I walked up to Jo's doorstep, stinking of aftershave. Jo had told me that her parents were away for the weekend, and her sister was staying overnight with a friend, but that didn't stop me from glancing around nervously. What was I doing that was so shameful? If someone I knew happened to pass by on the street, I was there to help her with her maths. That was it. Nothing else.

'Can I get you a drink?' Jo said once I had taken off my shoes.

'What have you got?' I asked.

'Pretty much anything. My parents are big drinkers. They're always stocking up, so they don't realise when things go missing. Wine – red and white – whisky, liqueurs (not that I recommend them). And there are a few cans in the fridge.'

I thought about this for a moment. Evidently, drinking alcohol wasn't something Jo reserved just for New Year parties. 'Do you have coke?'

Jo smiled. 'Sure.'

While I was waiting for Jo to come back from the kitchen, I took off my coat and draped it over the back of a chair. Jo had laid out her school stuff on the dining room table. A clean pad of A4 lined paper and two pens set out just like in an examination hall. I found this strangely comforting. She, like me, was keeping up the pretext that we were going to get work done.

I would just help her out, and then I would leave. It would be as simple as that. What was I worrying about?

Jo entered, carrying a coke and what looked like orange juice, although, knowing her, I suspected it had something else in it, too. She sat on the chair next to me and flicked back her hair.

'So, are we ready then?'

I drank a mouthful of coke. 'Sure.'

'Right,' she said. 'Algebraic equations...'

*'To work,'* I thought. *'To work, to work, to work.'* None of this confusion. I knew where I was with maths.

I won't bore you with the details of what happened over the next fifteen minutes. I've never come across an exciting plot based around maths, apart from *Pi* and *A Beautiful Mind*, but they were both actually about people going insane, weren't they? Basically, I worked through a few problem questions with Jo and didn't once have to look at the answers in the back of the book. I think she was impressed.

And yet, I couldn't help but feel disappointed. Maybe I had read the signs wrong. Maybe maths really was all that was going to take place here. She was using me, wasn't she? She only wanted me for my brain!

Had she realised that I'd caught hold of the wrong end of the stick? Did I have a one-track mind? How quickly I had turned from a clueless geek into a sex-obsessed moron.

Something touched my lower leg.

My first impulse was to lift the tablecloth to investigate. I wasn't aware of Jo having any pets, but I hadn't completed a thorough inspection of the premises.

No, no, those were human toes rubbing against my jeans.

'Please go on,' Jo said. 'I love it when you talk maths to me.'

I stared at her, mouth agape.

'You were telling me about cancelling out the exes,' she prompted. 'It was all very intriguing.'

Her foot moved further up my leg, past my knee and onto my thigh. Nobody had ever touched me there before.

'Um, yes, erm,' I said.

Jo smiled and placed her hand on mine. I had been illustrating my point with a diagram, but the moment she touched me, I let the pen go.

'I don't know about you,' Jo said, 'but maths really turns me on.'

Let me take a moment to acknowledge how uncomfortable this is to write – and, probably, to read. I was sixteen at this time, and Jo was fifteen. I find it disturbing now to think of us as sexual beings at that age. We were children, obediently following the steps that films and TV series had taught us. But awkwardness aside, it seemed completely normal at the time. In fact, it was considered strange for kids our age not to have had sex. That's how I remember perceiving it, at least. Now, how much of that was other people's bravado and illusion-spinning, I don't know, but I can assure you that it already felt that we had some catching up to do.

A fragment of time vanished. The next thing I knew, we were kissing. I've no idea how we got there or who made the first move, but it felt good, like a prophecy fulfilling itself. We were awkward at first, our mouths moving in different rhythms to each other, but we soon settled into it. Jo's tongue massaged mine. Her mouth was warm, and she tasted of vodka.

Kissing was fantastic! I had always feared it would be disgusting, with too much saliva and stray bits of decomposing food, but then and there, none mattered. Something on the path between my ears and my brain was filtering out the sucking sounds and lips smacking.

Jo's fingers were touching my face. I felt like I should

reciprocate, but I wasn't sure where it was decent to place my hands. In the end, I squeezed her waist.

My *you-know-what* was pressing hard into my jeans. The pressure increased until it was painful. I didn't get it. Weren't you supposed to get erect during, or just before, the act of sex – when it was acceptable? This was so obvious. The more I thought about it, the worse the problem became.

This kissing, this intimacy, was more terrifying than conversation. It was the intensity that got to me. Every movement, every adjustment of pressure, was significant and open to interpretation.

Just as I can't remember how the kiss began, I couldn't tell you how it finished. All I recall is that it was preceded by about thirty seconds of confusion. How was it supposed to end? I couldn't expect it to happen naturally – someone had to take the initiative – but what would it imply if I withdrew first?

Anyway, we stopped kissing, and the first thing I did was make sure that the tablecloth concealed the bulge between my legs. Jo's eyes were dancing. She watched me dreamily, smiling. God, she was beautiful.

'Thank you,' I said.

Jo giggled. 'That's okay.'

We stared at each other.

'I don't know about you,' she said, 'but I've had enough of maths.'

'It has its place.'

Jo leaned in close. 'I want to ask you, will you come with me?'

'Where?' I asked, although I would have followed her anywhere.

'Upstairs. To my room.'

I could barely believe what was happening. There was

no leeway for interpretation, was there? It wasn't as though she had a stamp collection up there that she wanted to show me. At least, I hoped not. That was precisely the sort of thing that would happen to me.

I had an image then of my mother. '*You're sixteen,*' she would have said. '*Far too young for that kind of thing. You're not old enough to know what love means.*' I had been paying less and less attention to her lately, though. And she needn't know. She never told me anything about her life. I was perfectly within my rights to reciprocate and hide something like this.

And I'm sure Peter would have struck me down, too, but I wasn't thinking about him.

Yes, I would go upstairs with Jo. There was no question about it: it was an excellent idea.

The only problem was that I could still feel my... organ straining against my jeans. What it may have lacked in stature, it more than made up for with enthusiasm. Surely, it was visible. What would Jo think if she saw it? Time for some quick thinking...

'I'm a bit cold,' I said, grabbing my coat off the back of the chair and draping it over the conspicuous region as I stood.

Jo looked at me strangely.

'Lead the way,' I said before she had a chance to say anything. 'I'm up for it.'

Jo's room was... interesting. It had that 'girl's room' feel to it: pink wallpaper and the cuddly toys lined up along shelves and windowsills, the smell of cosmetics and the dressing table mirror; tubs, tubes and bottles stacked up on the chest of drawers. It seemed so rich, like those mythic images of Arabia, with spices and women with shrouds that reveal only dark eyes and long, sleepy eyelashes.

Or it was an example of how fully many of us are constrained by the shackles of gender identity society imposes on us. You choose.

There was something more to it, though: evidence of a depth beneath teddy bears and *Maybelline*. Where most teenage girls would have had posters of *Westlife* or Orlando Bloom pinned to their bedroom walls, Jo had paintings. I discovered later that it was all her own work. The canvasses were a mess of sharp strokes, mainly dark in colour, with occasional gashes of red and yellow, random acts of savagery. I didn't know what she'd been thinking about when she'd done them, but I was glad I hadn't been there.

Another thing that really got me was the song lyrics and verses of poetry that she had transcribed neatly on bits of paper and blue-tacked to the window frame – innermost thoughts on display. I felt like she was bearing her soul to me, letting me in that room.

Jo raised her hands. 'This is it.'

'It's nice,' I said from the doorway.

'Come in.'

Jo didn't wait for me to move. She dived backwards onto her bed. Her hair fanned out artfully over the covers. I watched her chest rise and lower. She was so beautiful. What was I supposed to do?

I stood there, holding my coat over my crotch, and only started to edge forward when it became clear that Jo would maintain that pose until I did something about it. I moved close enough to look down into her face. Her eyes were closed. I wanted to touch her cheek, but the thought of it was too scary.

I squatted beside the bed and began to reach out a hand. I could feel her warmth already, an aura. I had never been this close to anyone.

I was way out of my depth. Sex had dominated my thoughts for years, whether I'd realised it or not. It had lost something of its mystery through being utilised to sell everything from shaving cream to fast cars, but none of that told me what to do in a situation like this. Worse still, it just emphasised the significance of it all. I had stopped being Nick, and she had stopped being Jo. We had become a statistic, a young couple about to be involved in *The Act* for the *First Time*. What should have been an intensely personal moment had become an Event.

Jo's eyes snapped open. She looked at me curiously. I could read her expression: '*What are you waiting for?*', but this didn't stop me feeling like I had been caught committing some heinous crime. I snatched my hand away.

Jo sat up.

I jumped to my feet. 'I'm sorry.'

'It's okay.' Jo patted next to her on the bed. 'Come here.'

We sat together for what seemed like an age. I felt oddly calm. My weakness had been exposed. Whatever happened next, it couldn't get any worse.

'Have you done this before?' I asked.

Jo laughed. 'That good, huh?'

'No. I mean, yes. Listen, what I mean is that you seem to know what you're doing. I don't. I really don't.'

'I know.'

'You know? How do you…'

'Put it down to superior powers of deduction.'

'Look, I'm sorry. I want to. Can we just…'

'Nick,' Jo interrupted. 'It's me. I like you. I'm not going to bite.'

I held my breath, awaiting the inevitable, '*Unless you want me to*', but fortunately, it never arrived.

Jo seemed to read my thoughts. 'Women don't say that

kind of thing in real life,' she sighed. 'This should be natural. Just do what feels right.'

I considered this before daring to look at her. The Jo I knew had returned. Gone was that perfect form, a fusion of fantasy and reality, which had so intimidated me. I could see the lines beneath her eyes, the honest roundness of her face, the hair on her lip, and the dents in her skin. I was with a person then, not a concept.

'What we were doing earlier,' I said. 'The kissing. That was pretty good.'

'Go for it, then.'

Jo shut her eyes and thrust her mouth forward, lips pursed, awaiting my next move.

I grimaced. 'You're joking, right?'

Jo grinned before plonking me one right on the lips.

And there it was. Somehow, I had got myself a girlfriend.

# Chapter 16

## *'I know.'*

elen stepped aside to let Peter in. 'What are you smiling about? I haven't seen you like this in months.'

Peter sauntered into her college room, beaming widely. It was morning, and the light was strong and fresh. Helen's room was always bright, courtesy of the tall windows and the walls, painted a neutral white (as students came and went) that perfectly befitted her purity. Her company lit up the place, too. There was something about her, something as addictive as it was captivating. And the smell... not perfume, not artificial... just sweet, like a childhood memory. She had made this rented space her own. Shelves were lined with textbooks, and a cross was pinned above her bed.

Helen closed the door and sat on a cushion in the middle of the floor, where she had a library book open. She looked up at Peter, curious, always interested and generous with her time.

'Come on then,' she said. 'Tell me what's up.'

Peter crouched and cupped his hands gently around hers. 'Guess. See if you can guess.'

'Come on,' she laughed. 'This is silly. It could be anything!'

'Could it?' Peter leaping to his feet, young again, despite having seen too much of the world. 'Could anything do this to me? Could anything make me happy again? Could anything bring colour back to my life?'

Helen frowned. 'I don't understand.'

'No, no, it's something you'll like! What's the thing you want most for me in the whole world? What do you pray for every night?'

Helen tilted her head to judge Peter from a different angle. 'You don't...'

'I do! I believe!'

Still, Helen retained that critical expression. 'I don't know what to say. It seems too good to be true.'

'It's not!' Peter said loudly. He felt like telling the entire city.

'How do you know?'

'How can you ask that? How could I not be sure I've been touched? How could I not realise the world has changed for me, that I've finally fought my way back onto God's path? It's all so clear now.'

After only a few more shreds of doubt, the harsh lines of Helen's scepticism melted away, and she was a girl again, imbued with all the beauty the world had to offer. She let out a little giggle, jumped up and hugged him. She had never done that to Peter before, had barely even touched him, careful to maintain personal space. At first, he was thrown off guard. Then he remembered that he had yearned for this as long as he had known her.

'I knew He would find you!' Helen shrieked, for she was as excited then as Peter. 'You needed Him so much!'

'I know. I'm so glad to have finally found Him. It's like a huge burden's been lifted. All that uncertainty. I'm finally accepting that this is the way things are. I realise now that He's been with me all along, waiting for me; I just never allowed myself to recognise Him.'

'I'm so happy for you.'

Helen withdrew from the embrace. They were still holding hands, but it wasn't awkward because neither of them was thinking about it.

Where did their thoughts lie? What dwelled behind that flutter of words and the exchange of glances? Had Helen taken Peter at face value, or had she already begun to worry that maybe this all fitted together too well? Peter's account of what it was to walk with God was too fully formed and expressed a little too well. His words sounded familiar: snippets of things she had said to him. Was his faith recycled? Had he deceived himself into it, and if so, to what end?

As for Peter, had he already begun to strain against the locked zones in his mind? Was he thinking that, finally, they lived in the same world, so there was no reason why they should not be together? Was he already considering his next steps?

'It's all because of you,' Peter said. 'You showed me the way. Without you, I would never have found Him.'

Helen loosened her grip, and Peter's hands fell to his side. It was the smallest of motions, but it could not have held more significance to Peter.

'God was always there,' Helen said firmly. 'You just had to accept him. That was your choice, not mine.'

Peter shook himself. A voice in his head rebuked him:

'*Yes, yes, of course it was. Stupid mistake. You can't tell her yet.*'

Another voice took a different line: '*You shouldn't be thinking about her at all. Your allegiance is to God now. You will take a woman only if He permits; only in furtherance of your service to Him.*'

How realistic was this, though? Peter's infatuation had driven him this far. He could not turn away.

He would leave it several weeks before making his move. Helen had to truly believe he had converted. That issue had to be laid to rest before he broached the other. It would be fatal to mix the two. She could not know his true motives.

In many ways, that wait was unbearable. Peter had worked tirelessly to obtain his faith, but he couldn't use it to get what he wanted. He had to pretend he was happier than he was. All right, so he had found God – that was great – but what he really wanted was her. One of the voices in his head kept telling him this was wrong. He couldn't make it shut up.

Helen started acting differently. Before Peter's conversion, she had always been available to him, prepared to answer every question, even the most revealing, with total honesty. Now, she was withdrawn, refusing to enter into meaningful dialogue and deflecting his enquiries with humour. She wouldn't talk about faith. Instead, she rattled off nonsense about books she had read or friends he had never met.

Peter had no choice but to accept this. Their relationship had changed, and they both needed time to adjust. He reasoned that his conversion had crushed the religious divide that had so conveniently doused the sparks between them. She was probably trying to return to her comfort zone, re-establishing the distance between them. Complete intimacy or complete isolation; it seemed apparent that there could be no middle ground.

Their relationship took a backwards step in other ways, too. Once again, her female friends accompanied Helen wherever she went, like Catholic school mistresses with sharp noses and half-moon glasses. They stayed close, defending her like a precious stone, attentive to her every need. Peter had to fight for her attention. He observed again the way that whole rooms revolved around her. Boys at the church lunches bowed, scraped and stuttered. He looked down on them but realised that he was little better. He lived every hour with reference to her. Days were marked triumphs or failures depending on whether or not he had seen her (bonus points if she spoke to him or looked at him in a certain way). This was all invigorating in a strange way, as long as he didn't think about it too deeply.

Peter could only take this for so long. Helen's entourage remained at her side right to the end of the church lunches, forcing him to leave empty-handed, having only exchanged a few words with her. He passed the time socialising with the male Christians while awaiting an audience. It seemed that everyone looked at him from an angle. At times, he suspected they knew exactly why he was there and that it had nothing to do with God.

Eventually, Peter decided that he would have to catch Helen alone in her room. This was far from ideal, but he didn't feel he had any other choice. He dreaded the prospect of psyching himself up to visit her and tell her how he felt, only to discover that she was at the library or out with friends. Maybe he feared a definite, too: uncertainty kept his dream alive. He wasn't sure he was prepared to take the risk, but dreams could not sustain him indefinitely.

Peter went there with nothing. No flowers, no chocolates. Their bond went way beyond that stuff. He wanted to disassociate this from the commercial trappings of romanticism. He was a man with nothing but love. His appearance reflected this, too. He wore the plainest clothes that day (his only jumper, salvaged from the back of the drawer, where it had twisted out of shape), and he left the house having neglected to shave.

The floorboards in the halls of residence screamed out with his every step. He wasn't a student. That much was evident to everyone.

The doors to the student rooms stayed closed, the faces behind the painted names remaining a mystery. Helen's door was as plain as the rest, identifiable only by the name beneath the peephole.

As Peter approached, that voice in his head piped up, telling him to stop, but he had learned to suppress this unfortunate side-effect of faith.

He knocked and waited, barely able to breathe.

As the seconds passed, the full significance of what he was doing began to dawn on him. Where once he had pictured a loving God and had associated faith with heaven and joy beyond imagination, now he sensed God's wrath. Peter knew plenty enough about sin and punishment, and had seen hell in Helen's pitying stare, but this was different. Was God's scope for forgiveness infinite? Could sins always be erased by confession? What if some lines could only be crossed in one direction, and the damned are forever damned and sinners forever steeped in sin? Was not a murderer a murderer for life, and a rapist a rapist in this world and the next? It seemed impossible to believe that a God as loving as Peter's could cut His losses with some of His children, but ruthlessness must be a natural part of divinity. What other explanation could there be for the world's miseries?

Peter heard the scratch of a peephole being uncovered. He tried his best to look natural.

Several moments passed before Helen opened the door. Was she weighing up the pros and cons of letting him in? Had they been reduced to that? He used to think that she understood him, that they had a special relationship... that maybe she felt the same but was afraid to acknowledge it. What if none of that was true at all? What if the forces twisting his intestines had also worked on his face, eradicating all individuality? Did she see him now as just an admirer, unrecognisable as a real person?

All those uncertainties vanished from his mind when he saw her.

'Hi,' he said.

'Hi,' she said.

'Can I come in?' Peter took a step forward before Helen had a chance to answer.

Helen closed the door a little. 'I don't know.'

'What do you mean?'

'I'm just not sure if it's a good idea.'

'Is there someone in there?' Peter pushed against the door.

'No!' Helen wedged it in place with her foot. 'What are you doing, Peter?'

'I just came round to see you.' Peter hadn't even told her how he felt, and already it was going wrong. 'Listen, Helen, I really need to speak to you. There are some things I need to tell you.'

Helen nodded. 'Me too.'

'Please let me come in.'

'I think we should stop meeting each other. It's not healthy.'

Peter felt suddenly light-headed. 'Why?'

'If you've found God, you don't need me.'

'But I want you.'

'I know.'

With that, smiling wanly, Helen closed the door.

The next few hours were a haze. Peter vaguely remembered standing dazed, rooted to the spot. Then, he was shouting and hammering at the door. Then corridors reeled, footsteps tumbled, and cars screeched, honked and growled. He fell through the streets, fleeing from everyone.

What had he done?

*'You serve only your filthy lustful body. Where will it lead you, Peter? Where did this weakness come from? Does it sicken you, as it should?'*

Peter had obsessed before, but he had never felt such shame.

That was the day Peter found his spot by the river, where he was finally alone, way out of town. It was there that he began to weep. Never before had he cried so freely. His anguish knew no limits. Destructive and liberating, it marked Peter's death and rebirth. His face turned blotchy, and the creases in his skin set in, forever to remain.

How had she done this to him? Why? She had promised so much, only to snatch it away. How callous was that? She was a cruel, heartless bitch. Pure on the outside, stinking rotten inside. She was as bright and distant as the winter sun. He couldn't believe he had been drawn in. More than anything, he wanted to expose her.

But he was too weak for that. She had destroyed him.

And she... wasn't Mary. He could have loved his wife. She could have borne his children. He could have seen that in her. And he could have lost himself in that. But that bridge had been burned years ago. He had made his choice.

How many wrong turns had he taken? What would he pay for the sum of his sins? All he had now was God, and he was unworthy even to utter His name.

Peter tried to get up, but he fell like a wounded animal. He reached out for a helping hand that wasn't there. A jogger looked at him strangely as she passed on the towpath, but she didn't stop. Just another drunk.

'*You're pathetic,*' the voice told him.

He tried again to stand, and again until finally he succeeded. He couldn't see through the tears, and he knew that he could not escape his misery, but still, he scrambled through the dirt, headed he knew not where.

'You must throw yourself on his mercy,' he told himself.

The voice controlled his mouth now; its words were his.

He wiped his eyes, thoughts rusting. Guilt, sin, repentance. He slowed, and his mind slurred, and those words were all. He fell to his knees and prostrated himself in prayer.

Finally, Peter's Lord had found him.

# Chapter 17

## *The Papers*

Life was good. Everything was flowing in the right direction. This was an entirely new experience for me, and I found it off-putting, to be honest. I was happy, but in an edgy, hysterical way, forever fearful that I had strayed into a tangent universe that would implode at any moment, spitting me back into real life, haunted by reminiscences of what might have been.

It was all going so well that I relegated the worst bits of the previous few months to the back of my mind and thought only about the future, like a sinner absolved of his crimes. The slate had been wiped clean; there was no point looking back. I got on well in lessons and regained the ability to concentrate. I started to enjoy the company of my friends. Where once their eccentricities irritated me to the point of distraction, now I just rolled with it. I gave Michael back his depressing CDs and invested in some of my own; I went to Sam's social gatherings whenever exam revision (and my calendar with Jo) permitted; and Brian, well, I had time for him, even though he mainly talked about TV programmes. I knew that if I listened long and hard enough,

I would catch patches of honesty. Somehow, I had discovered the patience to do this.

I forgot about Peter. This wasn't a conscious choice – it just kind of happened. If I'd have sat down and thought about it, I would probably have forced myself to keep going back, if only out of a sense of obligation. I had saved his life, so it was up to me to make it worth living. But he had nothing else to give me now, and I always had better things to do than listen to him ramble. Sometimes, this was homework; at others, it was going to *McDonald's* with Jo, and still others, it was TV shows. I wouldn't remember about Peter until afterwards, when it was too late to do anything about it.

This all makes me sound heartless, I realise. That's not the right word for it, though. 'Detached', that was it. I was more detached than before. I had stopped investing all that much of myself in anything. I just allowed myself to go with the flow. All that mattered to me right then was that I was happy.

Okay, maybe that does mean I was heartless.

This change in outlook was the result of two key developments. Firstly, there was the Jo thing. We decided pretty quickly that we were 'going out'. As far as I could tell, this gave me the right to hold her hand at chess club and pester her on the phone after school. There was this closeness thing, too, this expectation that we should share thoughts and feelings. Jo confessed that she had fancied me for months. She told me she hated chess and that I was the only reason she went. She talked about cold shivers and fleeting glances, about corridors bustling with people slowing in deference to me. The only way I could think to respond to that was to kiss her.

We did stuff together as a couple, too. Jo was keen on

salsa dancing. She had been itching to try it for ages. Her sister went regularly with her boyfriend, but Jo had never succeeded in finding a partner. How could I refuse? So, there we were, as saccharine as couples get, tripping over our feet and whispering sweet nothings into each other's ear (often at the same time). I was useless. My attempted flourishes were flailing limbs. I wasn't built to dance, and I had spent the best part of my adolescence making as small a play of my body as possible. The notion of using it to express myself was anathema.

But I persisted for the sake of the relationship. And I suppose it was fun, in a way. Being with Jo was fantastic. Finally, I had a girlfriend. It was like being given a membership card to an institution upon which society had laid its foundations. All of a sudden, I could get a handle on a load of concepts that used to be a complete mystery. I could begin to fathom the basics of intimacy and devotion, of how the simple act of inserting one sexual organ into another could breed togetherness. Not that we ever did that.

I loved being with Jo. More than that, I loved how she made me feel about myself. Just the knowledge that someone cared about me... I never wanted it to end. Words flowed freer, even when Jo wasn't there. I could no longer see any need to worry about what other people thought of me. Jo was living, breathing proof that someone could like me just the way I was.

The second key development that January was Mum. She started coming home earlier from work. She told me they had taken on a new intern, making it easier for her to get away from the office, but I reckoned she'd made a New Year's resolution to spend more time with me.

We took down the Christmas tree together. Normally, putting it up was a family affair, but it hadn't been that year

– Mum had done it whilst I'd been in bed. It had been bizarre to wake up to find the living room transformed into an Aladdin's cave of riches. Tinsel was draped around every door and picture frame, and fold-out decorations hung from the ceiling. Mum had done up the tree splendidly, with gleaming baubles (all brand new), spray-on snow and clip-on robins, all evenly spread. It had been the perfect Christmas tree.

But it hadn't been *ours*.

Mum had treated it with a spray, but the needles still dropped by the shedload when we started taking it down. She was ready with the *Hoover*, though. It was a team effort. I plucked the tree's fruit, and she wrapped it and stashed it away for next year. We shared out the candy sticks and chocolate Santas hidden amongst the branches.

We ended up with this carcass of a tree, stripped of all its riches, and two boxes of decorations destined for storage. It was usually my father's job to lug these up the ladder to the attic, but I stepped into his shoes with relish. Something about attics spoke to me in the same way that large, hand-carved wardrobes stuffed with fur coats appeal to every child who grew up with the *Chronicles of Narnia*. That journey into the unknown, where birds scrabble and pipes squeal... was an adventure. I mention this in the past tense because excitement has turned to trepidation now that I'm older. I haven't been the same since I watched *The Exorcist*. Scrabbling birds have transformed into demons lurking in the dark; squealing pipes now echo the screams of tortured souls.

When I came back from putting the first box away, Mum was unpinning the stockings from above the fireplace (or, more accurately, the sill above the gas heater). Her back was turned to me, and I couldn't see any evidence of tears, but I knew she was crying. There were only two stockings to take down that year, not three.

'Are you okay, Mum?' I asked.

My question hung there just long enough to turn uncomfortable. Then, Mum turned to me, smiling wistfully.

'I remember when I was expecting. We never actually intended to have you. I feel awful telling you that, but honesty's important between us. I never regretted having you, not for a moment. It was the happiest moment of my life, finding out I was pregnant.'

I didn't say anything. I guess I found it upsetting to find out that I was an accident, but I didn't feel unwanted. I was mainly reflecting on the fact that the trail of encounters that resulted in my existence was pretty tenuous. A brief exchanged glance, light angled onto a face just right, eyes meeting again moments later and lingering; chance happenings and chemical reactions. I was born out of a string of coincidences. When it came down to it, I was only me because the sperm cell carrying one-half of my genetic information outpaced its companions in the race up the ovarian duct. It's quite possibly the only competition I've ever won.

'I didn't know how to tell your father,' Mum continued. 'I knew he wouldn't react well, so I tried to soften the blow. I left money-off vouchers for nappies pinned to the fridge and wrote lists of boy and girl names out with magnets, hoping that – subliminally at least – it would prepare him.'

I sat down on the sofa, unsure where she was going with this.

'What's going on?' I asked.

Mum held my gaze for so long that I felt sure she would say something, but all she did in the end was chuck the stockings into the remaining box.

'Never mind,' she said. 'It's nothing.'

I smiled bitterly and muttered, 'So much for honesty.'

'Well, what do you expect me to say?' Mum demanded, eyes ablaze. 'Things are complicated. You can't rely on me to explain everything to you anymore. I'm trying my best. Really, I'm trying, but your dad is gone, and you'll probably never see him again.'

'That's all I wanted to hear.'

I was overcome by this big bundle of feelings: joy, pain, solitude, rage, regret; they all struck me in the stomach. I couldn't remember feeling like this before, and yet there was something familiar to the sensation. I realised that I had been choking this stuff down, denying it, living a half-life, anaesthetised, blinkered. That was gone now, that protection, stripped by our words. I'll tell you what it was like: when you go up in a plane, and your ears clog up with pressure, everything's muffled and distant. And then your ears pop, and suddenly, with a rush of sound, you're there again in the midst of things, with people all around you talking, snoring, and babies screaming. It was a shock to have regular service resumed.

Perhaps that's why it didn't last long. The shutters came back down, returning me to my detached world. I looked at Mum. What should I have felt? I wasn't angry with her – she was as much a victim in all of this as me. I wasn't angry with my father, either. Maybe I should have been, but I wasn't. What did it say about me that I didn't care about him enough to hate him?

I just wanted it to be over. I just wanted a family that I didn't have to tolerate. The way things were headed, maybe we were getting closer to that utopia. Maybe cutting my father out of the picture was the solution to all our problems. And Mum was telling me this as though it was a failure on her part. I wanted to tell her it wasn't her fault it hadn't worked out, but I couldn't for some reason.

One thing that the whole affair taught me ('whole affair'? – I'm talking now about the union that spawned me, yet somehow, I can't treat it with more respect) was that everybody's flawed. Perhaps I was unusually slow to arrive at that conclusion, but truthfully, I had operated under the assumption that my parents', or at least my mother's, outlook on things was always straight and true. It took their divorce to make me realise that the assumptions about the world they had bred into me were their own; they weren't universal truths. With that, I realised that everyone in the world is like me, trying their best, often misguidedly, to do the right thing. There was no good or evil, no absolute right or wrong, just a continual balancing act.

Peter would never have agreed with me about most of that, but I knew it was true. All because I had seen my mother's weakness. Not sin, but weakness.

As flawed people, Mum and I hugged. That was the first time I remember this happening since my father hit me. We held each other for ages, and when we finished, our relationship had changed. I was still her son, and she was my mother, but we were also equals.

The following morning, she got out the divorce papers. She'd had them for weeks, apparently, unsigned. She'd taken them out several times while I was in bed but never got any further.

We sat together at the kitchen table. Mum took a pen in her hand, but as she touched it to the paper, the nib wedged in an invisible rut and would not budge.

She glanced up at me.

'Do you want me to do this, Nick?'

All the muscles in my body suddenly tensed.

'Forget that,' Mum said immediately. 'This is my decision. None of this is your responsibility.'

With her left hand, she took mine. With the other, she signed the paper.

* * *

So that was it. Papers signed, bonds severed. I could forget about my parent's marriage. All those doubts and woes counted for nothing in the face of that document.

Should it have had such power? It was only a legal document and didn't prescribe any particular arrangement when it came to me. It certainly didn't decree that the links with my father be severed, but I took it that way. I didn't want to think about him anymore.

All right, so I might miss some things about him: his hearty laugh, brusque hugs and how he made me feel on those rare occasions when he was proud of me. I tucked those things away in memory. They were inconvenient. I was on a mission to cut all the grief out of my life. If some things had to be sacrificed to that end, so be it. It was like cleaning the crap out of my bedroom: sure, I might later regret binning the occasional cherished item, but that wasn't a concern right then.

My relationship with my father ended with so much unsaid. I can't tell you what in particular I think we *should* have said to each other, but there should at least have been some discussion about what all this meant. It was as much a question of whether I was fair to my father as whether he did right by me. Whatever the final apportioning of guilt, the truth is that we owed each other more. He was my father, and I was his son.

Now that I'm older and time has untangled the threads

of these events, I have less sympathy for my decision. I let him leave my life because it was expedient. I didn't want to face him and how he made me feel. Fast-forward to the present day, I haven't seen my father in years. I've no idea where he is or what he's doing. Come to think of it, I've no way of knowing if he's still alive. None of this mattered when the memory of who he was and what he did to us was fresh, but something tugs at me now, more than just curiosity. Ties of blood transcend reason.

But that is now. Back then, the conclusion of my parent's divorce was another example of my life getting back on track. I've thought a lot about the texture of lives, the idea that people go around in their own worlds, rationalised in ways unique to them, and with colours painted onto objects unique to each set of eyes. For me, that texture had changed. I was still me, but everything and everyone seemed different. I was happier and shallower than ever before.

# Chapter 18

## *Natalie*

I should probably have had an idea what was going on when Mrs Turner, our Head of Year, interrupted our French lesson. She was usually the bounciest of the teachers, constantly harping on about challenges and achievement, and egging people on to get involved in the Duke of Edinburgh awards. That day, she had a solemn look on her face. She tiptoed into that classroom and whispered into Madame Godin's ear. She was careful and restrained; gone were her gesticulations. I watched Madame Godin's expression change from its customary Gallic aloofness to mild concern.

If I had been my usual morbid self, I might have guessed what was happening. Instead, I glanced quizzically at Michael (we shared a desk in the middle of the class, being neither conscientious enough for the front row nor sufficiently rebellious for the back). He shrugged at me.

Madame Godin instructed the whole class to go immediately to the assembly hall. We weren't alone. We bumped into Sam's psychology class in the corridor. It appeared that our entire year had been pulled out of lessons. Everybody was very excited.

'We don't get enough of this,' enthused Alan Turner (one of Sam's 'intellectual' friends). 'It breaks up the day; keeps us on our toes. I bet you don't get anyone complaining they're bored in earthquake zones, where you dive under your desk at the slightest tremor. Last time we had that kind of excitement over here was the Blitz.'

I laughed, but I wasn't really listening. Alan was playing it cool, acting like he didn't care what was happening. I didn't have patience for that. I wanted to know!

The caretakers had stacked all the chairs away in the assembly hall to make room for the afternoon's drama classes, so there was nowhere to sit. The noise was unbelievable: the clamour of the school field trapped within brick walls that rebounded every sound. The louder it got, the louder we had to shout to be heard. Imaginations ran riot. Our teachers would normally have silenced us, but they, too, were talking amongst themselves. Mr Spencer, the headmaster, was there too, chatting with the deputy head. He was wearing a grey suit, and he looked wearier than ever before.

As soon as the last class had filed in, Mrs Turner and Mr Spencer mounted the stage. At once, all the teachers from our classes let loose a blanket coverage of 'shssh'.

Mr Spencer seemed unusually nervous. He unfolded a piece of paper and then gripped the podium for support. We weren't used to seeing him like this. He always did his assemblies entirely from memory, ambling freely from one end of the stage to the other.

'There are times,' he read, 'when it falls to me to announce upsetting news.'

There was definitely something in his voice. Not firm

anymore, not authoritative, but soft, just as it had been when I was sent to him that time.

'Last Saturday, Natalie Powell, who I know was a friend to many of you, was involved in a traffic accident. She was taken by ambulance to Addenbrooks where, although she fought bravely, she passed away in the early hours this morning.' Mr Spencer paused and looked up at us. 'I realise that this news will come as a terrible shock.'

He was right. I barely knew Natalie, and yet I could feel myself getting choked up. Mr Spencer might have tried to soften the blow, but in the end, his news came down to the word 'was'. Death had struck someone I knew. It was no longer something that just happened to older people. It was immediate; it was a threat.

You probably don't remember who Natalie was. I don't blame you. If she hadn't died, I probably wouldn't remember who she was either. I last encountered her on New Year's Eve, when she hugged me and congratulated me for punching her ex-boyfriend, Sean, on the nose. That was the high point of our relationship. Before that, I'd had her pegged as one of the key players in the group that bullied Brian. It seemed churlish to hold that against her now.

I had all these preconceptions about Natalie: that she was one of those who think they're the only ones living life to the max, with their clubbing, socialising, smoking and underage drinking. I imagined (quite accurately, it tran-spired) that she had been mown down when staggering across the road in the early hours at the end of a heavy night out.

It's funny how the things we associate with living life to the fullest are, most commonly, those that kill you.

'School will continue today,' said Mr Spencer, 'but if

any of you feel you need time away from class or want to pay your respects to Natalie, then I encourage you to do so. Make use of the quiet rooms in A-block. If you need to go home, please make sure you get the go-ahead from your form tutor.'

So, we were stuck at school. One of our number had passed from this mortal plain, yet we were still stuck in lessons. I couldn't help but wonder what it would take to get a school day cancelled. Bad weather hadn't once kept us at home that year. The school curriculum wouldn't bow even to death. Now, that demonstrated a real commitment to the league tables.

I noticed that Natalie's closest friends hadn't come in at all. Sean wasn't around, either. By coming into school, we had identified ourselves as only loosely acquainted with her.

Still, death seemed to bring us together. News of Natalie's passing struck us all. We didn't separate into our usual cliques that day. Ours was a kind of communal mourning. One thing I'll never forget was the silence. We communicated mainly in glances: brief eye contact to check that someone was all right; the response was an exaggerated happy, sad or indifferent face. Why we didn't talk, I don't know; it just seemed inappropriate. Perhaps we were reflecting on the fact that we're all mortal and all things must pass; perhaps we were all just too shocked to put energy into anything we said. I felt a greater kinship with my peers that day than ever before or since. It was as though they had all strayed temporarily into my world.

The same did not apply to the people I usually called friends. We assembled after school, having planned one of our swimming trips. By then, we were all feeling lethargic, our energy sapped by spending the day in an environment where it would have been a sin to smile a millimetre. We abandoned the pool and took instead to kicking our way through town, headed nowhere in particular. The weather was still miserable, right at the tail end of January. The Christmas holidays seemed to have ended ages ago, yet spring wasn't even a pinprick on the horizon.

'Well, that was depressing,' Sam said.

His words had the effect of disintegrating the protective shells we had formed around ourselves. Suddenly, it was far easier to speak.

Brian followed up quickly. 'Bug on a windscreen, that's the way to go. I couldn't hack one of those lingering, painful deaths. No, one second, you're alive, then bang, you're dead, that's the way to do it.'

He cared, didn't he? Only a little, but even that was surprising. It wasn't all that long ago that Natalie had played a part in making his life a misery.

'Think of the mess, though,' Michael said after a moment's reflection. 'Someone's got to clean it up when people hurl themselves off buildings or jump in front of trains. God, I hate the idea of my body just being this pile of sludge that someone's left to shovel up. Going that way, it's just so inconsiderate. Think of the hassle. Like with bugs on windscreens, it's impossible to get them off. They stick like cement.'

We could all identify with that, having been employed by our parents at various points over the years to wash their cars for a bit of pocket money. I remember one time my hand was so stiff from scrubbing the remains of insects off my father's windscreen that I had trouble writing the next day.

'Cement?' Brian scoffed. 'Cement doesn't stick to anything.'

'What about polystyrene cement?' said Michael.

Brian wrinkled his nose. 'That's not your conventional glue. I doubt it would stick to a windscreen.'

'Michael sighed. 'Okay, they stick like glue. Whatever. That's what I meant.'

'I don't think it was,' Brian said. 'I don't think you'd thought that far ahead.'

'I almost got run over by a *Mr Kipling* truck once,' Sam said, averting what would otherwise have devolved into a lengthy debate. 'Didn't look where I was going and walked right out in front of it. Can't say my life flashed before my eyes, but it was shocking, all right. I was lucky – it would have ruined my street cred. I can just imagine my death certificate now: 'Cause of Death: *Exceedingly Good Cakes.*' It doesn't bear thinking about.'

The three of them giggled about that for the next ten minutes. I couldn't join them. It was nice to hear laughter, given how the day had gone, but at the same time, I couldn't help but find it callous. A girl had died, after all. None of us had particularly liked her, but she still deserved a bit more respect.

Death wasn't real to them, even then. They had died a thousand times in computer games, only to be resurrected from the last save point. They had watched their heroes cheat death in movies, and seen men and women slaughtered in service to a plot. The films we watched dwelled little on the aftermath of death. Just like them, we moved on to the next thing.

Not me. I couldn't stand it. As the subject changed to *Warhammer Fantasy Roleplay*, I trailed behind them a few steps. When they turned a corner, I seized the opportunity to about-face and walk the other way. I was long gone by the time they noticed.

I made my way to Queen's Road to pay my respects. I

had heard through the grapevine that this was where Natalie's accident happened. I wasn't sure how reliable my sources were until I got to the Backs, where I saw the makeshift memorial erected against the fence at the end of Burrell's Walk. There were cards pinned to the wood, and bunches of flowers stacked against it. January's frost would make light work of them, turning petals black and limp beside the weeping ink of the photo of a once vibrant girl.

I stood there for a while, gazing down at the flowers. People from my year came and went, leaving cards and notes. They didn't say anything to me. When they were gone, curiosity got the better of me, and I crouched down to look at the messages. Grief, to me, was always a private thing. I couldn't understand how writing down your feelings and displaying them publicly could be therapeutic. Who, or what, did it serve? It seemed odd to leave a testament to how Natalie's death affected them next to the cold, miserable road that had killed her.

The process of writing this account has helped me understand this better. I've had to pick apart my adolescent mind and impose order on thoughts that weren't so clearly defined at the time. I've had to explore my motives and fears, and piece together a narrative. In a funny way, externalising this stuff has helped put much of it behind me. Pieces of paper scored with real, solidified thoughts are more readily discarded than memories. I'm probably being unkind to those who left tributes, but it must have been at least a part of what they got out of it.

I didn't leave a message of my own. Instead, I reflected on all the things that Natalie would never experience. I had no idea what she might have done with her life and who she might have touched, but she had already fallen one formative event behind the rest of her year group: she had never experienced the death of a peer. With each day that passed, the list of things she had missed would grow. She would always be trapped, aged sixteen.

I remembered Natalie from school corridors and the New Year's party. I would hear her chatting with friends, telling them that she wouldn't change as she got older, that she would still wear fashionable clothes and enjoy clubbing, and that she couldn't see why age should change this. I remembered her pale, ash-flecked skin and overzealous laugh that crunched her face up like a walnut. All those memories had a peculiar echoey quality, as though they were rattling around in a massive, vaulted chamber. Somehow, they had become precious. I still look back on those moments with reverence, an inexplicable awe, given what little she meant to me when she was alive. She emerges from scenes now, the only colour in a monochrome world. Death has granted her a substance that she lacked in life.

And yet, the manner of her death seemed so pointless, so futile.

I turned from the memorial and walked along the Backs. The night had set in. A layer of frost had already formed on the windows of parked cars that were still pinging as their engines cooled. The temperature's rise and fall had shattered a discarded beer glass filled with rainwater. I should have headed home before it got colder, but I knew what I had to do, and it would not wait. I had to find Peter.

How long had it been since I last saw him? We had parted amicably, I suppose, but this was probably only because we hadn't intended to part at all. Given the urgency that gripped me that night, it seemed like madness how I had forgotten about Peter. I needed him desperately right then. Only he would be able to understand how I was feeling. He lived apart from this society and could see beyond the next working day to the fate that awaits us all.

I sought him first in Midsummer Common. It was where we usually met, and I knew he studied there often. Nothing. The streetlight by the old towpath had burnt out, so I could barely see the bench. I fumbled in the darkness to check whether he was there, but no, it was empty.

I headed then for Parker's Piece. Maybe Peter was preaching again to commuters stuck at the traffic lights. I jogged there. My breaths rose as clouds in the air. Still nothing.

I stood for a while outside the toilets, in the spot where Peter preached. I resolved to venture down the part of Christ's Piece behind the bus station. I had heard talk at school of 'tramps' and 'junkies' who slept rough there, occasionally jeering at passing kids.

Peter might well have been beneath those low-hanging trees, but I was too frightened to look closely when it came to it. It was pitch black, but for the copper light that oozed through the misty bus shelter glass, so it was next to impossible to make out any faces. There were quite a few bodies around – I could tell this from the occasional rustle and hushed voice. Sometimes, mounds of earth became human and sat up to look at me, like the undead emerging from the grave.

I said nothing. My jaws clamped tight. I couldn't open my mouth to ask after Peter. Just because he and I had a friendship didn't mean that I had forgotten who I was and who these people were, and that, for better or worse, there were many reasons why our worlds didn't usually touch.

It hit home that night just how big the difference is between rich and poor in Cambridge. I was searching for a man who owned nothing, pushing past shivering tourists and late-night shoppers laden with bags of gifts they had bought for themselves. The colleges, too, reeked of opulence. They stood proud every which way I turned, with their ancient masonry and limestone steeples jutting into the sky, the product of patronage lavished on them by kings and lords.

In the gaze of history's spoilt children, *Big Issue* salesmen plied their wares to passers-by, who tried their best to blank them; beggars pleaded for loose change to buy a cup of coffee to warm their fingers; and an old woman rooted through rubbish bins for scraps to eat. It made me feel sick, seeing people living like that on my doorstep, knowing I had tacitly accepted it just by living my life.

What was it about this place that attracted them? Was it the 'bright lights' and expectations that they could extract money from Japanese tourists? What had they found here instead? People too tight to give, or wary that their kindness would be frittered away on drugs and alcohol? I once saw someone pause from begging to take out a mobile phone and tell his wife what time he would be home for dinner. People like him made life that bit harder for those that depended on people's goodwill.

I stopped on the spot, realising that I knew where Peter would be. I remembered the Bible he lent me and the logo on the inside cover. There was a night shelter in Cambridge. I couldn't remember the address, but I could look it up in a phone book.

I sneaked into the University Arms hotel and located a directory by the phone booth in the lobby. The night shelter wasn't far. It was beneath one of the city's churches and wouldn't take long to walk to.

It hadn't yet opened its doors when I got there. People were queuing up outside, eager to secure a place out of the bitter cold. I couldn't make out Peter among them, but if I waited, maybe he would come.

I sat on the wall across the road from the church. Cars streamed past continuously, separating me from the crowd and making me feel safe. The church, though by no means monolithic, had a certain gothic appeal, virtue of the plastering of muck from exhausts. The entrance to the night shelter was thick and grey, with a tiny window of reinforced wire-mesh glass. I became tediously familiar with every detail of that building's surface as I waited.

This was an endurance trial. I cupped my hands together to breathe warmth into my fingers, and swung my legs to keep the blood flowing. I wasn't dressed for this. I still had my school uniform on, and those polyester trousers were thin and cheap. It didn't seem like I had any padding on my bum. The bricks were in direct contact with bone. The air itself jabbed at me.

The night shelter's tenants were faring little better. Their coats were frayed, and their woollen hats had large holes where the stitching had given way. How did they cope with being outside all day? I just couldn't get my head around it.

The doors opened at about seven thirty, and everyone filed in. Still no sign of Peter. I was pretty sure I hadn't missed him. I was about to go over and ask after him, but my joints had seized up, and I had this uncontrollable desire to get home. Tremors racked my insides; I could feel my whole body quaking. I couldn't go home like this, though, and face the interrogation my mother would put me through as she nursed me back to health.

I opted instead for Jo's. I sprinted there. My heart was pounding like anything. Mum would have killed me for taking that kind of risk, with my condition and all. I wasn't thinking straight.

'Come in, love, come in,' Jo's mum said.

She ushered me towards a radiator and shouted upstairs for Jo.

Jo came down in a man-sized T-shirt. It looked like she was getting ready for bed. 'Where have you been?'

I was still struggling to breathe, so I didn't respond. My vision was cloudy, and my ears rang.

Jo proceeded instead to peel off my clothing, explaining that the heat would get to me quicker that way.

Jo's mum went into the kitchen and came back with a glass of brandy. 'Drink this.'

I turned my head away.

'I'll take care of him, Mum,' Jo said.

She ushered me up the stairs to her room. I collapsed on her bed, curling up in a ball and shivering. Jo put her hand on my brow. She hugged me, trying to warm me up. I didn't respond.

'Are you okay, Nick?' she asked.

I looked at her and nodded slowly. She smiled at me and went downstairs. The next thing I knew, she thrust a mug of hot chocolate into my hands. I held it to my cracked lips and inhaled the steam.

'Is this about Natalie?' Jo asked. 'You two didn't date, did you?'

I raised my eyebrows. 'Me and Natalie?'

'Well, I don't know! I've never spoken to the girl. I don't know if she's got standards!'

I wasn't entirely sure what Jo meant by that.

'I spoke to her at New Year's,' I said. 'She hugged me. Now she's dead.'

'I hope the two are unrelated.' I don't know what

expression crossed my face then, but it made Jo change tack quickly. 'It's very sad.'

I looked at her, trying to piece together the fragments of my thoughts. 'I don't think I knew her... I'm not mourning her... I don't have any right to. It's like I'm... grieving for myself... for all of us... we've all got to die.'

Jo took my hand, and we sat silently for a few moments. Did she understand what I was talking about? Could she comprehend the full implications, the inevitability of death? Not the intellectual concept, the reality.

'You know what I'm afraid of?' she said eventually. 'People not remembering me. I hope the people whose lives I touch will remember me when I'm gone, but it's not enough. There will come a time when those who remember us have passed on. Then all that's left of us is a name and maybe an epitaph. Maybe part of me lives on in my great-grandchildren, passed on in genes, but it's diluted; it's not me. I'm long gone. And moments like these are gone. And the warmth we share – your hand and mine – is gone, too.'

I looked at her, my girlfriend. This beautiful, intelligent girl was spending this time with me. She only had a finite amount of it to invest, but this, this was mine, this was ours.

'I know exactly what you mean,' I said. 'I'm afraid of wasting time... of not living life to the full... of not realising my potential. I want to leave a mark on the world, but... It's like life is a burden... like we have a responsibility to make the best of it.'

'You're here with me,' Jo said brightly. 'That's a good start.'

'It is,' I smiled and kissed her. 'Thank you.'

# Chapter 19

## *The Journal*

I didn't look for Peter again. The thought just never really came up; it never resurfaced. Peter was one of many things vying for my attention. He lost out to the pace of days. All too often, the most important choices we make don't present themselves as choices at all. Day-to-day life is just an illusion to distract you from what really matters.

What mattered to me then was Jo. I was utterly and completely in love. I couldn't stop thinking about her, anticipating the next time I would see her, and planning out conversations we'd have. These flew out of the window when we met, of course, but that didn't matter: when we were together, we never lacked stuff to talk about. There was this incredible link between us. I shared things with her that I had never expressed to anyone, even Peter, and she understood. I told her what had been happening at home. She didn't have any answers, but that in itself was refreshing. Peter had an explanation for everything, and it was always God.

My days got bolted down quickly. I was always with

someone, be it Jo, Mum or my friends. Revision for my GCSE exams began to take over, too. I spent every spare moment studying, cramming my head full of information.

I still woke every morning among books I had read for Peter, accumulating dust. I should have recognised the clues that I was missing something and leaving a story half-told. There was a message in the hollow eyes of Natalie Powell's close friends and in the winter air that pervaded, but I didn't want to hear it. I was moving on. I did so without having resolved anything, just like I was doing with my parents' divorce. Peter had become a figure from my past, just like my father. They still wielded power over me, tempered by distance perhaps, but power nonetheless; I just didn't want to recognise it.

A month passed. Winter still gripped us firmly. It was late February, and snow threatened. I rushed home from school to avoid the weather. Mum must have had the same idea because when I opened the front door, I saw her coat hanging in the hallway. I deposited my bag at the bottom of the stairs and set about extricating myself from my scarf. Mum must have heard me come in because she shouted, 'Hello, love' from the kitchen.

'Hi Mum,' I said as I joined her.

Mum had her laptop out and had spread papers across the kitchen table. I didn't bother looking at them. Mum rarely brought work home, but what little I'd seen of it had seemed interminably dull: all figures, flow charts and official-looking reports – the worst elements of school. I made a beeline, instead, for the biscuit tin on the worktop.

'Not so fast,' Mum said before I was even halfway there.

What, was she going to tell me to wait until after dinner? I was a bit too old to be warned about spoiling my appetite! I drew in breath to object, but Mum simply turned her face, indicating that I should kiss her on the cheek. All right, I supposed I could deal with that. A minute later, I was enjoying a ginger nut.

Mum was looking healthier than she had done in years. Her hair was tied back, but her face didn't look as stark as usual. There was roundness there, and colour. She had rolled up her sleeves, revealing no injuries or bruises.

I was about to engage in another raid on the biscuit tin when the phone rang.

'Oh, that's probably for you,' Mum said. 'A man called earlier, asking for you. Wouldn't say who he was.'

I went through to the hallway and picked up the receiver.

'Hello?'

'Nick Farlowe?'

'Yes.'

'Hi, my name's Geoff. I'm calling from the night shelter. I don't suppose you know someone called Peter Williams?'

'Peter?' I paused, unsure whether it was wiser to confirm, or deny all knowledge. 'Yes, yes, I do.'

Silence. I discovered later that Geoff had phoned all the Farlowes in the directory. Now that he had finally contacted me, he didn't know what to say.

'I'm afraid I have some bad news...'

I carried on listening, but my brain disconnected from Geoff's words. I knew exactly where this was going. Deep down, I recognised that I had abandoned Peter and that there would be a price to pay.

The death of Peter was as inevitable as the turn of the seasons, yet I still relied on the wall for balance when the news hit. I sank slowly to the floor as Geoff uttered syllables without meaning, so struck was I by the enormity of fate.

* * *

During his final weeks, Peter was driven by a greater sense of purpose than ever. Everyone in the night shelter – staff, volunteers and residents alike – noticed the change in him. Where often Peter would make a nuisance of himself, sitting at the table furthest from the television and commenting loudly on the day's events, in his last weeks, he retired to bed early to scratch at his journal with the stub of a pencil. Where once he would start a fight by imposing his views on an audience that neither sought nor appreciated them, now he kept himself to himself. This made him no less unpopular. The other residents read aloofness in his manner. And his nocturnal habits irritated those with whom he shared a dormitory. He continued his work long after lights-out, scribbling and muttering to himself and granting others' complaints the honour of nothing more than a grunt.

As time passed, grumblings turned to ultimatums. The occupant of the bunk below complained to the night manager that he couldn't sleep because of Peter's sporadic splutters and spurts of dialogue. The night manager took Peter to one side and brought this up as diplomatically as he could. Peter was never one to accept criticism. He accused the staff of being instruments of Satan, sent to discourage him from Christ's path. He collected together what little he owned and stormed off. They never heard from him again.

Peter set up camp behind the bus station, but this place didn't serve his need for solitude, either. Other rough sleepers kept attempting to make conversation. He ignored them, but they didn't take the hint. This was their community; they had a right to question him. The background noise, too, was a challenge – the hiss of hydraulics, the endless drone of engines and passengers boarding and disembarking. Such distractions bogged him down, preventing him from attaining the spiritual togetherness he needed for his task.

The boy had stopped coming to see him. It could only mean one thing: God had released him from that task to concentrate on the next. Peter's journal was to be his testament. The path to complete it had been cleared. He just needed to rid himself of all distractions and let God's will take over, flowing through his arm, down to his fingers, to the tip of his pen.

It was not so easy. One afternoon, Peter glanced up from his work to see Helen waiting for a bus. For one blissful instant, he really thought it was her. She looked slightly different from how he remembered, but that was only to be expected. How long had it been since he was last in her presence? He couldn't even remember.

This woman was in a business suit. Black-framed glasses rested on the bridge of her nose. Was she on lunch break? Peter couldn't picture the Helen he knew working in an office. Her faith would have driven her on missionary work to the poorest countries.

No, this wasn't her.

Still, Peter closed his notebook and gazed at the woman through the glad of the bus shelter. He couldn't help but notice how sad her eyes appeared and that her forehead was creased. He could not know what troubled her, but he could feel her loss. Peter watched her discreetly, subdued by her presence. She was the only human being to have moved him in an age.

Her bus arrived, and Peter scrambled through the bushes to keep her in sight. He couldn't miss any of this. His eyes followed her as she took up a window seat.

These moments would be the only contact Peter would have with this woman. She didn't even know he was there. Her life would remain forever a mystery. He resigned himself to that, but the bus doors stayed open too long. Heavy seconds pounded, keeping their connection alive.

Peter drank her up. For a moment, he loved again.

Then she was gone.

Hours later, when darkness descended, Peter was still there in that same spot. Countless buses had come and gone since then. School kids had queued, awaiting their ride home, and then the rush hour had got underway. Peter took none of this in.

What had he done? Once again, he had failed. He was the same man he had always been, still capable of the same mistakes. He could not purge himself of lust. He remembered trying to force himself on Helen all those years ago. That crime would forever taint him. It hadn't been a temporary insanity, but a manifestation of his very nature. He was filth, and God couldn't cure him of that. He couldn't control his eyes, couldn't stop them from probing every inch of a woman's body. The only solution was to pluck them out, those sinful globes.

Yet lust had brought Peter to God. He had followed Helen into church, had entered the presence of divinity, just to be close to her. His infatuation had driven him to make her world his own. It was still strong enough to keep drawing him away.

The only solution was to isolate himself.

Peter followed the river out to the wilderness. This place was a sanctuary to him; he had fled here before. It was where his God had found him, and it was there that he would stay.

They hadn't yet felled the split tree. Fungus had taken

hold of the flesh exposed where it had pulled itself apart, reaching for the heavens.

As the days passed, Peter adopted a routine. During the daylight hours, he hid himself in the brambles beside the towpath, fighting through thorns that shredded his already tattered clothing. He felt like a child again, making a den, a place of his own in a time of relentless change. He cleared the faded crisp packets and empty aerosol cans. Mud plastered him. The ground wasn't quite cold enough to solidify.

Peter endured all of this. If there was one thing he could do well, it was endure. He focused on his work. It would all have been worth it if he could forge something positive out of his pitiful existence. God had put him through trials to prepare him for this task. With his Lord as his muse, Peter's words would save souls.

Why, then, did God forsake him? Peter had done everything He had asked of him. Yes, he was an imperfect vessel for the Holy Spirit, but that was why he had gone there, to the wilderness, away from temptation. The words should have flowed naturally. Why was every line laboured, every sentence imperfect?

In frustration, Peter crossed out entire paragraphs and ripped out pages.

At the end of the first day, Peter's stomach objected. For hours, it had growled. This turned into a sharp pain as the sun set. Peter curled himself up, bent almost double. Only then did the discomfort recede.

It came as some relief when the last light faded from the sky because it meant it was no longer possible to write. He crawled out of the brambles and stood, straightening his stiff back. Blood returned to his extremities and, with it, sensation. At once, he began to shiver. He paced back and forth to warm himself, rubbing his hands up and down his arms.

When it started to rain, he took shelter beneath the motorway bridge. Tremors overtook his body as he knelt, slurping up the water that accumulated in the concrete gulleys.

Peter slept fitfully, tucked up under that bridge. His bones ached, and the blanket with which he covered himself did little to stave off the cold. The stabbing pain in his stomach returned. His one relief was that his skin had turned numb, so he felt little discomfort from the concrete. The first effects of hypothermia, familiar now, began to ease in.

When he woke the following morning, his tongue was sandpaper. The rain had ceased, but water was still dripping from stalactites of concrete sediment. He shuffled into a position where he could intercept them with his mouth.

The shakes returned soon after that, uncontrollable this time, a hundred times more violent. They made it next to impossible to catch the water. Most of the drops landed on his beard or his face. The few that fell in his mouth tasted of chalk. They did nothing to quench his thirst.

'*This is pathetic,*' he thought to himself as he shook. '*Is this what it's come to?*'

'*Of course it is,*' he countered immediately. '*All God's servants must be tested. And it should be so. Did not Christ suffer ten thousand times worse than this? To follow Him is to follow to the end.*'

Peter pushed down the part of him that demanded if it had all been worth it. There was anger, too, a primal rage against the prospect of death. Deep down, despite everything, he wanted to live. Something reared up inside him: a final rush of life on the eve of death, like the last burst of affection lovers feel as a relationship fails. He beat this down as he would a rabid dog.

Above him, the sky rolled on. To Peter, it was time itself, constantly in flux, charged with such energy and emotion. The romance of sunsets, drenched in pink and purple; the cloudless nights, embellished with the fires of failing stars; black winter sapped life; summer storms warned of God's wrath. Peter rolled over to admire the beauty of dawn, of rebirth. The horizon was white. It was difficult to tell where the colour began. White merged to grey and then imperceptibly to fragile blue. The sparse clouds were gold and set in soft focus. The sun battled through branches and lingered low in the sky, a flag sailing at half-mast. Day by day, this act had played for millions of years, yet the colours were still as fresh as God intended.

It was all the more magnificent because Peter knew this dawn would be his last.

He dragged himself back into the bushes and lay there as his shivers subsided. A couple of hours later, he lost all movement in his legs. He kept writing as long as he could, but his fingers eventually seized up. It didn't matter much by then because his vision was a blur.

As the short day drew to a close, it began to rain again. Peter wept. His tear ducts were dry, yet still he wept, thanks to the bramble leaves depositing their load onto his cheeks, nature's final courtesy.

'*Is this it?*' he asked God, although his tongue could no longer form words. '*Has all my time been wasted? I haven't changed anything.*'

It had the quality of a final thought, but it was not Peter's last. As he closed his eyes, too weak to stave off the weariness any longer, he was gripped by loneliness. He told himself that he needn't fear death, that Christ was always with him, but still he doubted. He sensed that the end was near, and it seemed to him like a house fire, when all those photograph albums and trinkets collected over the years go up in flames, a whole lifetime of memories wiped clean.

Perhaps that's what they mean when they say your life flashes before your eyes. Maybe the neurones responsible for memory fire up one last time. Images are replayed as the slate wipes clean. One by one, experiences are lost to infinity until even the most cherished moments succumb.

I sometimes wonder what you must do to be the final thing that flashes before someone's mind's eye. Will I see my mother or father, my first love or the woman I marry, people I have yet to meet, or children that have not yet been born? And Peter, what did he behold in those dying seconds? Did the years fade to nothing until he was arm-in-arm with his wife? Did the memory of Helen plague him once more? Or did he relive the moment when his life truly changed, when he witnessed for the first time God's anger? Did he see a caravan tugged through the mud towards a cliff edge? Did he see it plunge once again into darkness?

For the first few days, I felt ill all the time. I sat in front of the TV all day, not really watching it or taking in any of the words, just trying to distract myself. Everything anyone said to me caused a pain in my head. I couldn't bear to be in the same room as other people. Unconsciously, I think I was trying to imitate my mentor, his ordeals and his eventual demise. Peter's death had finally dragged me into his world.

A fog still descends on me whenever I think back to when I was told that Peter was gone. The world gets colder. My emotions intrude, and I feel such bleakness. Depression is a picture frame. It changes the context of everything.

At the time, I was convinced that it was my fault. Peter's

demise was unequivocally linked with the carefree way I was leading my life. The connection couldn't have been clearer: I was with Jo when I should have been with him. As Peter withdrew from the world, I was parading through town hand-in-hand with her or breathing onto my bedroom window and painting love hearts in the mist. Never had my actions held such consequence.

I had failed. I had only managed to prolong Peter's life; I hadn't made it worth living.

Now, of course, I recognise that none of this had anything to do with it. Peter had set himself on that path long before we met. He was always dying. A switch had flipped in his brain, making that inevitable. I had just delayed it a bit.

I had to tell my mother. There was no hiding this from her. She was all over me as soon as I put down the phone. 'Who was that?'... 'Why is someone from the night shelter ringing you?' She could tell that I was upset. I told her to forget about it and shut myself in my room, but I could only hold out for so long.

I spilled it to her about half an hour later, when I realised I couldn't cope with it alone. I told Mum about the night I first met Peter, about his death, and how it was my fault. I made no mention of the Bible studies I undertook at his direction. She would never understand that and would ask too many questions. Her God wasn't Peter's.

I knew it had been the right decision to withhold this when I saw the expression on her face. She didn't need to make any motherly comments or chastise me for taking such a risk; she didn't need to emphasise the 'strange' in 'stranger'. It was all there in her expression: morbid terror, inconsistencies clicking together, the realisation that she had allowed this to happen. She sat at the dining room table with her head in her hands. Occasionally, she looked up at me as if to check that I was still there, that I was real.

'I'm sorry,' I said.

Mum didn't respond. She wasn't helping. I didn't know what I had expected of her. But at least it was all now out in the open.

We never spoke of it again.

That weekend, I cycled down to the river, to the place where Peter died. Everything seemed to lead back there. It was where I had come closest to God, but at the same time, it was laden with other associations. The split tree, with limbs flailing madly for the heavens, was Peter's tombstone. A solitary bunch of flowers had been left there by someone from the night shelter. Only five or six people had signed the card. How did this compare with the collective outpouring of grief over Natalie's death?

I hadn't taken anything myself. It seemed far too early to acknowledge Peter's death in that way, to mourn him, to fit how I felt into any kind of customary grief structure. When Natalie died, I hated the way everyone jumped on it and marched down to her memorial with flowers purchased from petrol stations and supermarkets. The residue of commercialism made everything two-dimensional.

I sat against the tree, opened my backpack, and pulled out a leather-bound book. Its cover was stained with rain. Peter's journal. He had left it for me. My name was written inside the front cover. I hadn't read further yet. I had been putting this off for days.

A few months earlier, I would have given anything to discover that book's contents. I remembered the care Peter took over it. I used to try stealing glimpses over his shoulder as he wrote, only for him to snap the tome shut and regard me in that disapproving manner that came so naturally to him.

This was Peter's only gift to me. Its words were all the more precious now that he was gone. The significance of that was difficult to ignore.

It was the hardest thing in the world, opening that little book. I crossed my legs and set it on my lap. I flipped open the front cover quickly, like I was ripping off a plaster. I was slower and more delicate with the inner pages.

The reverence with which I held this book dropped away after I started reading. The first few paragraphs said it all. Despite the paper's dampness, the graphite letters stood firm with the authority of a monastic text.

*This is the account of Peter Williams, a disciple of Christ. The Word was flesh long before I was born to this earth. I write in an era when man recognises only that which he can touch, a time when God's existence must be proven.*

*Christ still speaks to us, but few listen. Even I was deaf to his words until my later years, when I freed myself of worldly matters. Unshackled from Satan's manacles of ambition and animal impulses, I heeded Christ as he spoke to me of Judgement and of forgiveness. He gave me one task. He instructed me to spread His word to the heathen, to appeal to their twisted reason in language that they would understand. He granted me the gift of visions; divine revelatory ideas, which dissolve as dreams if I do not solidify them here. In this, my Gospel, I set them down for others to study.*

*Christ is coming. Heed my words.*

. . .

It carried on that way for pages and pages, extended tracts about revelation and modern-day sin. Peter had an opinion about everything, and disgust for all that humankind strived for. I read it all. It was difficult to follow at times. Peter's thoughts were disjointed, and they often contradicted each other. He never linked new ideas with what had gone before. The only common thread was self-righteousness.

I wasn't sure what else I had expected. This was Peter; these were his words, and I could picture him saying them. Yet somehow, seeing them written down made me study them differently. Peter's teachings no longer benefited from the force of his delivery. Laid out on the page, stripped of all that, Peter's faith was exposed as that of a desperate, fractured soul.

He mentioned me further on:

*And a boy named Nick came to me, and I instructed him. Day and night, he battled his demons; day and night, Satan clouded his vision with petty concerns. And then, the education and upbringing that had so blinded him gave way, and Christ strode in. And lo, the boy glimpsed the light of divinity.*

That was all Peter had to say about me.

The rest was him, all him and his Christ. There was no narrative, and little of what he wrote bore any relation to his current reality. Even towards the end, as Peter's handwriting deteriorated into a spiky mess, he made no direct mention of his intention to close out his life. His words simply became less flowery, more direct, and he dwelled on the legacy he would leave. Did the Holy Spirit so possess him that he neglected everything else? Did he not realise he was killing himself as he pushed his body to its limit?

How much of this was Peter, and how much of it was his God? Was this truly what his God intended, and if so, to what end?

There were so many questions. This book held no answers.

# Chapter 20

## *Yesterday's Shadow*

Dawn creeps in through net curtains. It's not magnificent, just plain. The windows in the council flats opposite reflect a concrete grey, the grey of yet another working week, of a city long overdue sleep. I didn't notice the first stirrings of this new day because I've been sat up all night at my desk, writing under the glare of an angle-poised lamp. I couldn't watch the sun rise over trees and fields because I'm stuck here in London.

In many ways, the years since Peter's death have been eventful. The summer that followed the events I've recounted witnessed me sweltering in exam halls, sitting my GCSE exams. I did well enough to stay on through sixth form, where I decided that (in the absence of anything better to do) I would pursue further study. I got a place at King's College, London, where I studied theology. The extra-curricular activities Peter had encouraged me to pursue became the bread and butter of my day. His influence on me lasted, although not in the way he would have wanted. Degree-level theology was an academic exercise. Faith was irrelevant. Christianity remained rooted in a past so fantastical, so steeped with history, that miracles flooded the air. Gods inhabited ancient trees and crucifixes bleeding in the sunset. Divinity pounded at me within cathedrals, towering architecture designed to dumbfound, but nothing sprung within me.

University was a liberating experience. I was my own boss, living away from home. Mum sometimes dropped by after work (she commuted into central London), and I stayed with her in Cambridge during the holidays, but otherwise, I was on my own. I tell a lie – I did share a flat with three others, but we only crossed paths in the kitchen while heating up ready meals. They hogged the TV, watching *Hollyoaks* and *Who Wants to Be a Millionaire?* I didn't join them.

I got on well with the others on my course. We met up often, studying together or going out for drinks. Occasionally, they managed to drag me out clubbing with them. We're still in touch. Vaguely.

I can't say the same for my school friends: we don't even have 'vague' contact these days. We pretty much forgot about each other come the end of sixth form. It was too much of an effort to stay in touch after that. Our contact was sporadic, mainly during holidays, when we returned to Cambridge, and we continued to keep in touch for a time on social media, but even that has faded away. We've become mere names in address books, and there's no reason to change this, to strengthen these bonds or sever them completely.

In our time apart, we became different people. Time mellowed us, filled us out and sand-papered away the quirky spikes of our characters; we've become more 'normal'. One by one, we discovered sex and slotted this into our mediocre understanding of the human condition. We backtracked through time to fill in the blanks – cultural events that we missed and non-sci-fi TV programmes that formed the basis of student conversation, which we might have shunned a couple of years earlier (yes, I'm talking about *Friends*). Finally, we began to fit in, each to a different circle.

Brian got a place in Clare College, Cambridge. I remember he was chuffed about this because it meant he could save cash by living at home. I was incredulous when I found out. If I had been in his situation, living in his brother's shadow, I would have snapped up the first opportunity to get away. Brian got into Cambridge, but he remained second best. Even so, the last time I heard from him, he seemed happy enough. He stayed in Cambridge to pursue a doctorate, and became well-known as a stand-up comedian at *Footlights*, specialising in mathematical jokes. According to the reviews, he can do things with Pythagoras' Theorem that will make you wet yourself.

Sam skipped university, choosing instead to work stacking shelves at *Asda*. We all thought he was insane, but he was convinced it was the way. While I was in lecture halls, he attended left-wing rallies. His latest *Facebook* posts include photos of him chained to trees, fencing, and the occasional statue. He talks about 'the worker' and 'the *proletariat*' a lot. Maybe he's plotting some kind of revolution… more likely, he'll harp on about bringing down 'The system' for another few years before taking out a mortgage and settling down with a wife, two kids and a Labrador.

Michael moved up to Leeds with his family. I didn't hear much more from him after that, but I did learn that he joined a rock band called the *Purple Pixies*, playing bass. They got quite big up there, touring bars and village halls. He turned his unkempt appearance into an asset. Take a deathly complexion and greasy hair, add sunglasses and a guitar, and you look the business.

Jo and I stayed together until the end of sixth form. We didn't last into university. Couples split up left, right and centre back then because everyone decided that long-distance relationships wouldn't work. Had it been just that, we would probably have stuck it out and seen where it took us, but our relationship had already begun to deteriorate. I've thought about it a lot and concluded that we expected different things from each other. Jo insisted that we share everything, every second of the day; I tried to maintain a distance. It was a miracle that she got as close as she did. I couldn't let anyone in. I felt like I needed to keep secrets, that they were all that made me interesting. If she were to know me inside out, I would instantly become boring. Jo called it an intimacy problem. But that discussion I had with her, freezing cold, after my failed search for Peter, that was what I wanted. I just couldn't face the idea of moments like that becoming commonplace, expected, even.

This whole relationship thing was too much for me to take in, anyway. I didn't feel like I understood the basics, and Jo and I were moving way too fast. We were together for over two years, a proper, established couple. She got on with my mother and even joined us for Christmas dinner. I don't think anyone would have been surprised if we'd have got married and stayed together the rest of our lives. The idea terrified me. Don't get me wrong, I wasn't entirely opposed to the concept. It was just that it seemed beyond my control. I felt like I had missed something fundamental, as though I had skipped straight to the black belt in karate, and it was only a matter of time before I would have to go three rounds with *Mr Miyagi*.

This was only to be expected. Up until the point that Jo

and I got together, the female figures in my life were peripheral at best. I loved my mother, but she was distant, and I couldn't pretend to understand her as a person: she was just Mum. At school, girls roamed in packs to protect themselves from the boys. The only time that barrier was ever breached was when people coupled. It was beyond me how one gender had enough contact with the other to decide that they wanted this to happen. Maybe they just woke one morning, and an innate biological need overtook them, and they just happened to come across someone with that same need at the same time, and that was that: they would merge, like two bubbles coming together in a washing-up basin.

So, yes, my only real experience of the opposite sex was my mother. Somehow, that was supposed to set me up to understand Jo. It was an impossible ask.

I remember one argument we had about me sending 'officious' text messages to her. Jo couldn't understand that texts aren't the ideal medium for expressing emotion. I think this was before emojis, but if not, I'd have had them on a banned list anyway. And towards the end, we had this discussion about Douglas Adams. 'How can you not want to read a book called *The Long Dark Teatime of the Soul*?' I demanded. 'I just don't,' she shrugged. Never had the rift between us seemed so vast.

But let's not dwell on that. We had a great time together, and I owe Jo a lot. It was her, more than anyone, that pulled me through the darker days that followed my parents' divorce. She was my first; to this date, she's been my only, and I loved her.

Who knows what she's up to now? She's probably married with kids; if we were to meet again, it would be as strangers. Why is it that, when it's over, we push away those we let get closest? Is the memory of tenderness unbearable?

Or is it that we can't stand the idea of someone getting to know who we truly are and deciding 'no, thanks'? That's not a concern of mine: the version of Nick that Jo came to reject is long gone.

I look back now at my life as a teenager with the benefit of nostalgia. It's more than that, though. Everything meant more then. As a child, I was new to experience, so everything was exciting. I remember taking the train from Cambridge to London for my first term at King's. I looked out over mist-clad fields, peering into woods and folds in the earth shrouded in white, and thought to myself that anything could lie there. The Earth was unexplored; there were still nooks and crannies that I could populate with imagination. These days, I know exactly what lurks around the next corner. It's all there in *Google Maps*.

Don't get me wrong, I don't idolise my childhood. I can look back and acknowledge that parts of it were crap. I've no desire to relive it. I just wish I could have carried more of the younger me into subsequent decades.

I have a job now at the council. Nothing related to my degree: I process housing claims, assess needs according to certain fixed criteria, and enter data into a formula to calculate who gets the next available property. People phone up and try to trick me. They cobble together complaints and crackpot stories, but they can't beat the system. It's too dull for words. I keep reassuring myself that it's good experience, which will help me career-wise, but each year that passes takes me no closer to wherever it is I want to be.

I've moved on from the days when I had a tangible goal in mind, be it exams, surviving university or leaving home. I concentrated so much on those goals that I didn't consider where they would take me. I drift through my days now without aiming for anything in particular. I can feel time slipping away pointlessly. It used to move slower. Childhood slips to adulthood and then to old age and death. If I don't catch hold of something, it will all be over before I work out what I'm supposed to do.

I have an uneasy feeling that the clutter that fills my life – domestic routines, bills to pay, people to meet, assignments to complete – is nothing more than a distraction from what really matters. I'm not sure what that is exactly, but I do know that the key lies in those months around the turn of the millennium. Without Peter, I am a million miles from the extraordinary.

That's why I've written this. I'm trying to take myself back there, to pick up where I left off. For a while, just after Peter's death, I tried to piece together a coherent picture of him from what I knew. It was an attempt to compensate for the omissions in his journal, to pull together an account with more flesh. I jotted down memories, recorded bits of his past that he divulged to me, and conjectured at his thoughts. I've incorporated pieces of this work into my account here.

I made contact, too, with others who knew him. The night shelter staff recognised my need to lap up everything I could of him and let me attend the wake they held in his memory. I shared a meal with the closest Peter had to friends. None seemed particularly bothered by his death, just aware of his absence. The nearest I got to a hint of loss was from this old boy called Paddy, the epitome of the 'older gentleman' stereotype: he wore a corduroy suit with a comb in the top pocket. He had been on the street since the Falklands.

'He was a character,' he said, rolling himself a cigarette. 'These days, you don't get many characters. Love 'em or loathe 'em, they liven up the place.'

None of this got me any answers. Peter was impossible to fathom.

This problem has proven to be perennial. Sitting down to write this account, I've focused much more on me than him. The Peter I portray is poorly drawn, a mere outline of a person. That's because the picture I formed of him is still bitty, with gaps as significant as the elements of his personality I never witnessed. What struck me as I put pen to paper was that I barely knew him. Everything he said was littered with passages from the Bible. Sometimes, it was impossible to tell where Peter ended and Christ began. Perhaps he wanted it that way.

The process of writing about Peter, assuming the role of his chronicler, has seen me stamp him with my character and perspective. I've found it necessary to fill in the blanks with assumptions shaped by my own beliefs. This is where this account falls down. How could I, of all people, possibly do him justice? For me, trying to understand Peter and pull apart his past is like trying to describe a tree without referencing the words 'leaf' or 'branch', 'green' or 'brown'. There is an essence to him that defies my ability to comprehend.

Peter's biography, his saint's life, will never be written. He tried and failed to do it. My attempt was doomed from the start.

What I have succeeded in doing, though, is taking myself back to those crucial months. I can see now what I lost. In amongst it all, what mattered were the questions that Peter made me ask, the truths I sought to find. I've identified the spirit that used to burn within me. The memory of Peter has rekindled it a little. This time, I'm not going to let it be snuffed out.

* * *

I couldn't sleep last night. The hot city air smothered me. I lay in the dark, my bed sheets damp with sweat. And in the early hours, it came to me, fear of death. I hadn't felt it in a long time, not that strongly. I lay alone, more alone than ever before. No one was there to comfort me, to hold me, to save me. I pictured my corpse in the ground, rotting away, and a black hole opened inside me. I saw through the petty concerns that fill my days. I saw that it is all superficial and cannot last. Everything I am, everyone I know, and everything I experience is just a smudge in time.

I had no faith to combat that fear. I wished I could believe in God and heaven, but they weren't real to me. They offered no reassurance. Death was grinning at me, and I had no choice but to accept it.

I did a strange thing amid this: I abandoned any attempt to comfort myself and tried instead to cling to the despair. I welcomed it. It was what I had been missing. It would spell the end to this half-life, to this unquestioning acceptance of things as they are. It's only fitting that I should feel that way because my life is advancing, every wondrous or mundane moment, towards oblivion. Better to accept it than blind myself with ignorance. Only by keeping my ultimate fate firmly in mind could I learn to make the most of what time I had.

I used to envy Natalie Powell. I envied her because she appeared to find fulfilment in the superficial. She faced death, ignorant of the stench that lingers over everything and everyone. Death must have caught her unawares. But how full had her life really been? I realise now that you need darkness to throw things into relief. You can't truly appreciate colour without having experienced night, health without disease, or summer without winter.

And Peter, he was the other extreme to Natalie. He let his faith dominate him and stop him from living.

But what did I really know of either of them? These are all just assumptions, true only in the little world I have created here.

Peter's decisions are dictated to him now by the written word. His life events are pinned down on the page, to be relived again and again with every read. He is trapped forever in events that rip at his soul. When Peter sacrificed himself to the elements, he ended any chance of escaping that cycle and consigned himself to the past. No matter how I tell it, Peter's tale will always be tragic. There is no hope for him.

Unlike Peter, I still have choices. For now, at least, I am still here. I live not just in the shadow of yesterday but of tomorrow. I still have hope.

# Also by P.J. Murphy

## Dead Letters

A year after the disappearance of bestselling author, Richard Debden, his ex-girlfriend receives the manuscript of his unpublished final novel. She shares it with a mutual friend, and together they delve into the text, recognising parallels between fiction and reality. The story contains messages for them and a trail that leads across the country and – dare they hope? – to Richard.

Also available as an audiobook.

## Troubleshot: A Satire

Troubleshot charts the plight of a village falsely identified as a problem hotspot, and a community that will benefit from public-sector support, whether they like it or not.